WHITE FIRE

AN EVE OF LIGHT STORY

HARAMBEE K. GREY-SUN

HYPERVERSE BOOKS, LLC

Cover design by The Cover Collection

Published by HyperVerse Books, LLC

PO Box 23642, Alexandria, VA 22304

www.hyperversebooks.com

Crossing genres without apologies.

Print ISBN-13: 978-1-64044-032-6

Ebook ISBN-13: 978-1-64044-031-9

WHITE FIRE

All of us in the bar died that night.

For only a moment.

Though how can one estimate an actual moment after suffering a kiss with oblivion, ceasing to exist?

Even before that hateful meet-cute, the minutes (hours?) had begun to blur as a small gathering of us watched the ball game playing on the two big screens. The Little League World Series. Two among the bar's joyous patrons claimed to be related to a couple of the players. One man claimed a step-nephew on one team; the other—a woman—claimed a cousin on the opposing team. As the two cheered and jeered, everyone else in the bar good-naturedly chose sides, splitting pretty much down the middle so that neither of the two had to root alone or in a significant minority.

I knew all about feeling alone. It was why I'd slinked into the bar in the first place.

An unattached paralegal in her midtwenties considering—dithering about, really—law school and all that would entail . . .

Did I really want to be a lawyer? Did I really want to be an exceptionally successful lawyer, putting my career before a potential family? Did I really want to commit before finding true love with a perfect match?

The ball game drew on, eventually ended. But the two dozen or so of us didn't wind down. There was a victory to celebrate and a loss to forget. More beers. More bourbon. More martinis.

At some crook on the boozy slide to utter drunkenness, *he* oozed into the joint.

Alone, I think.

A dark-skinned man in a black raincoat and fedora.

Whomever he was, he seemed determined to put a damper on our mood. His opening gambit was to shove his way between two men and a woman standing next to a booth, close talking. He appeared to be heading for the hallway that held the bathrooms, but he only glanced down the short passageway before turning sharply and heading for the end of the bar, the far end from where I was sitting.

Someone shouted that he should apologize. His apology was a rude gesture, flashed without hesitation as he continued on, slipping behind the bar and passing through the door behind it as if he owned the place.

The bartender, the lone man on staff in this cozy establishment, had been servicing a table but dashed for the bar the moment the man made himself at home.

Knocking a glass from another table in his mad rush, the bartender shouted curses and commands at the one who ignored him before he, too, passed through the door behind the bar and disappeared. I was sure the shouting and cursing continued, but I heard nothing.

Left on our own, we patrons were all good. No one tried to slip behind the bar to grab a bottle, bust the register, or even refill a mug from the beer tap.

But the bartender was gone long enough for glasses to go dry and for some of us to consider going into the back room ourselves, to coax or drag both men back out.

Before anyone could take initiative, a man emerged. Alone.

The surly one. The one whose eyes were filled with hate.

He breathed heavily as he stepped from behind the bar, glaring at all of us while some of us, a lot less cheerful and far more inebriated than before, hurled insults at him, taunted him.

He approached a pillar and circled it three times, each time scanning our faces as if searching for someone he might recognize. He then moved to a position closer to the front entrance, a spot where he could see all of us without turning his head more than a fraction of an inch.

Two of the bolder men, following an even bolder woman, approached him, intending to get in his face, maybe even forcibly eject him from the premises. But the man in the trench coat raised his left arm above his head, lazily reaching toward the ceiling, and the room fell silent.

Not voluntarily.

Speaking for myself, I felt unable to speak. The others' mouths gaped; their lips contorted as they tried to form words; they gestured toward their hands and throats as their eyes widened in surprise, narrowed in frustration; we all pantomimed to one another in frightened wonder, stomping, pounding tables, smacking wood and even our own skin in futile attempts to make the sounds our mouths wouldn't.

The televisions, still bright and running, were as silent as we were. Glasses dropped or accidentally knocked to the floor shattered without hiss or whisper.

Two from the trio—a man and a woman—who had been angrily approaching the man in black continued toward him with more energy, apparently determined to lay blows on him, maybe to see if he would make a sound or, even better, reverse whatever he'd done to us.

The man in black simply crossed his arms behind his back and seemed to get taller as his eyes flashed like suddenly struck matches.

The man and woman spun away from him like tops, crashing into tall round tables and stools before tumbling to the floor. All spectacle, no accompanying sound.

Panic increased among us. Some dashed for the hallway, perhaps hoping to escape through the bathroom—a window or emergency exit—or maybe just hoping that their ears would actually work if they put more distance between themselves and the instigator.

But they never found out.

Stools, chairs, and low and tall tables that hadn't been nailed down rose and flew through the air faster than any bird of prey, clogging the hallway's entrance.

Those who'd dashed for the bathrooms or whatever else might be found through that limited passageway pivoted and headed for the bar. Like the two men who'd proceeded them, they slid behind it but found the door to the unseen back locked.

Amid all the quiet pandemonium, I performed my own frantic yet ultimately useless dance, stumbling here and there, destination unknown, and remaining near the bar as a result, never straying farther than the closest table. As aimless as my legs, my eyes darted to and from each of my fellow inebriates, hoping to land on one who might have a solution to our predicament. In their course, my eyes landed on the source of it all and lingered as I noticed he hadn't gotten taller but was levitating, hovering now at two or three feet off the floor.

Others who noticed this slowed their leg and arm movements to gaze at him. Maybe, like mine, their thoughts became more animated than their bodies—bodies passing through the air, smacking into objects, without noise . . . My—and perhaps their—thoughts screamed into a void.

The few who weren't focused on our captor, those who were still searching for exits, suddenly stopped and gazed like the rest of us when the man deigned to speak.

"I came in here looking for something that was stolen from me. I was told it was in a back room. But the fool I just interrogated told me that he put it in one of your drinks. And one or more of you willingly swallowed it."

Reflexively, some of us looked to our empty glasses as others placed a hand over their stomachs, as if their palms or fingers had hidden eyes that could see through clothes and skin.

"Well," the man bellowed, "now that you've all heard me clearly, I'm going to give you a chance to fess up. Which of you elected yourself a celestial mule? Raise your hand."

Some of us exchanged glances. One or two shrugged.

"Okay, I'll try another way. Which of you drank the liquid of silver? The elixir with red ice?"

I'd had a few margaritas made with a tequila whose brand boasted of silver—but surely that couldn't have been what he meant.

But the expression my thoughts put on my face captured his attention.

With a sneer, he approached me, walking on air, gradually lowering himself to the floor. "You . . ."

My limbs stiffened. I couldn't step backward, couldn't turn my head as he neared, his sneer contorting into a grin.

"You've got something on your mind."

My heart kicked. Each throb sent a sensation of searing heat or intense cold through my entire body. In spite of these flashes of extreme temperature, I still couldn't move. Couldn't even close my eyes when the man brought his face within inches of mine, his irises glowing, burning like miniature suns with beyond-black holes at their centers.

Before everything blanked out, I had a sense that someone else was in the bar. Someone who'd rushed in through the front door.

When I next knew sensation, I knew I'd been intimate with oblivion.

The sensation had been on my eardrums (or thereabouts). A small-voiced string of words. A long incomplete sentence, sung. Its end hung somewhere my ears couldn't find, compelling me to use another sensory organ.

Before my eyes opened, I knew I was lying on my back in wet grass, naked. My skin, slick all over with dew, I presumed, as my bleary eyes rapidly focused on a colorful sky, a bouquet courtesy of a rising sun.

I wasn't alone. My barmates were with me, equally naked and glistening, in a relatively flat field that seemed to stretch on forever no matter which way I turned as I—wincing, whining, grunting—pushed up to a sitting position and eventually got my feet under me.

My first thought was the afterlife. We had awoken in limbo, or in an anteroom to Heaven. Or a lobby of Hell. On that we couldn't agree—that is, after all the initial screaming and shouting and other exclamations of fright and confusion were over with.

We had our voices again, and we used them to pollute the slightly violet-scented atmosphere with panicked and angry clouds of noise. Beyond ourselves, nothing was roused. There were no birds that I could see. No land creatures. A few skeletal trees in the distance. But nothing else.

After our gathering had calmed enough to where only three or four of us were still sobbing, two or three still cursing, and two—only two—still hollering at the top of their lungs for someone beyond our group and beyond our sight to respond and offer a hope of assistance, we managed to agree that we weren't dead, but very likely had been. We weren't in an afterlife, or on another world, but still on Earth. And we'd better gather our wits and determine which direction to go if we were going to make it back to civilization.

Despite none of us being—or admitting to being—as cold as we should have been, we each felt some degree of chilliness. Moving became more important than reaching a consensus.

We split into three groups heading in three directions; two of those directions were generally toward where we spotted the most trees.

The ground was moderately uneven but thankfully not rocky. I and those in my group moved as quickly as we could to keep from shivering, though the weather wasn't as biting as it perhaps should have been. Judging by the state of the grass and the leaves on the trees we approached, it was likely November, or even early December. The Little League World Series had been in August.

As my group progressed and what had been a relatively flat field to the eye became noticeably less so, it occurred to me that none of us were self-conscious about our nakedness. But then we had other things on our mind, other topics on our lips.

Our conversation eased away from where we were and worries about making it home to a debate on what had actually happened in the bar, who or what that man had been, and how much time had really passed since that evening.

We reached no satisfying answer on any question but we were delighted—our excitement warming us even more than the climbing sun—when we found ourselves at the top of a hill, looking down on a gravel road about one and a half lanes wide. Farther in the distance were rows and rows of grapevines. To our left, we saw that the road wound in the direction of a barn, a house, other structures.

We'd happened upon a vineyard.

Carefully, we made our way down the hill and walked by the road's side until we were at the point where we could leave it and walk in nearly a straight line to the house's front porch.

It was then that three of us—two women and a man— became worried about our state of nakedness. But there was nothing to do about it. This was no movie scenario where sheets and various garments were conveniently hanging on a nearby clothesline. We had no immediate options open to us other than to choose the least visually intimidating among us—a woman, naturally; me, specifically—to ring the bell and knock. I covered my breasts with one arm and used my free hand as a fig leaf. The others stood off to the side near the driveway, out of the line of sight of the door's peephole and all adjacent windows.

After two more rounds of ringing and knocking, wide green eyes peered through the left sidelight window. Soon after, the door creaked open just enough to give view to an older woman —just her head, and just enough for me to judge, by her eyes and wrinkled brow, that she was concerned and cautious in equal measure.

She looked me up and down. The expression in her eyes changed so suddenly, I expected her to threaten to call the police or to pull the door open wider to reveal she was wielding a semiautomatic.

Instead, when she pulled the door open wider, I saw nothing but a middle-aged woman in bathrobe and slippers extending a cell phone to me.

"Call who you need to."

No one came to my mind. No one other than the several ones congregated near the driveway, each of them trembling, likely experiencing their own unique fears of the future and anxiety about our recent shared past.

I gestured in their direction. The older woman saw and made her own gestures, distantly herding my companions—and me—toward the garage door. She disappeared inside the house.

Within five minutes, the garage door opened. Inside, a high pile of blankets rested in the back of a pickup, placed there perhaps by the woman with the assistance of the lanky and equally wizened man who hovered near her by the steps leading inside the house.

The woman and her companion were clutching cell phones. Both asked us whom they should call on our behalf. A spouse? A significant other?

When we asked and were told we were in Virginia—far from the Pennsylvania bar in which we'd experienced our last joyous moments—we opted for ambulances.

Some openly mulled calling the police; others wondered what we would tell them without being written off or possibly arrested as a bunch of crazies. I decided that we had no choice but to involve them. At the very least, we had an obligation to tell them about the other groups.

It wasn't until later that evening that I began to feel some sense of order returning to my life.

Paramedics had checked most of my fellow wanderers at the vineyard before the police escorted them to various locations. I opted to go to the nearest hospital for a more thorough examination. It was there that I reconnected with the others from the field who'd gone off in different directions.

One group had made it to another vineyard. The other group found itself lost in the woods for a bit until some hunters spotted them. I decided that we all should keep in touch once we'd all made it back home and gotten resettled into our respective lives.

And we did. Though the number of us who kept in touch dwindled over time.

I imagined that everyone except for me had friends, family, and other assorted loved ones waiting to welcome them back after their three-months' disappearance. Me, I was thankful I didn't own a pet. Only several dead houseplants and a refrigerator half-stocked with spoiled vegetables and expired milk awaited my arrival.

The local authorities were happy for our reemergence but were no closer to solving just what had happened at the bar that night. After we blanked out, the place was destroyed by a fire. Arson. The bartender's was the only body recovered.

Some authorities vowed to stay on the case—but what exactly was the case now? The missing persons had been found, and they had no memories of what had happened to them after the antagonistic man had entered. And all of us— every single person who'd been in the bar that night and had lived—struggled with describing the man. Not a one of us could remember his face.

As we kept in touch, we tried to help each other remember. We tried to help each other with a number of things. But it seemed we were just fighting losing battles with ourselves.

We discovered that each of us had been awakened by a different string of sung words. Not only was this knowledge unhelpful, it also increased the anxiety of some, pushing them closer to the edge of their own sanity.

I'd my share of breakouts. Rashes. My skin experienced a range of blemishes until, after uncounted months, it began to even out. An even tone that, at times, seemed to glow. On rare occasions, a few tiny spots—here and there—would glisten. On rarer occasions, there'd be many more scintillations, confusing me. If dark spots portended cancer, what did these mean?

All of us experienced recurring nightmares. Many of us

experienced a range of seizures—a periodic shaking or jerking of body parts, sometimes culminating in a loss of consciousness. Some developed Tourette syndrome or something similar to it.

More than a few eventually succumbed to suicide.

Me, I started therapy. Early. Pretty much the day after I made it back to my lonely apartment in Pennsylvania. Talk therapy. Physical therapy. Medicinal. Many therapists. All manners of drugs and treatments. Much of it funded in one way or another by my very understanding employer that, miraculously, did not fire me.

I worked for a white-shoe law firm that apparently had greatly appreciated my paralegal work over the years. And over the next several, I managed to keep myself together well enough to go to law school and secure a job as an associate at the same firm.

I was making it through. I was on my way.

I even made it to my wedding day.

I married my therapist. One of my many therapists. Which one exactly I didn't remember. His face I didn't remember. His words, I did.

You must cultivate—endeavor to cultivate—self-love. That had been his mantra. His repeated advice to me.

Among his many suggestions of practices that might help, I took to dancing. *Really* took to it. Dancing alone, as a way to wind up for or wind down from some of my exercise routines (different dances, depending on how I was trying to manage my heart). During one session with the man, when I rose to my feet to demonstrate what I'd been trying to explain, he eventually rose from his chair to join me. Soon after, I was no longer managing my heart on my own.

Corny and weird to think about it. Corny and weird was the ceremony. Parts of it.

The fact the ceremony had taken place on a verdant, oceanside cliff was a mixture of corniness and weirdness. I'd no background to merit such a setting, had never even as a young girl imagined desiring one for my happiest day. But there we were, elated, beaming, the briny scent of the sea reaching us—all of us —me, my partner, and our two hundred or so guests composed almost entirely of his friends and associates. A smattering of my coworkers made up the rest of the attendees.

Salty breezes aside, the air was suffused with glittering specks, motes of dust igniting to be consumed in tiny, silent sparks when the early afternoon sunlight hit them just right. My eyes were drawn more to the flowers.

The spectacular colors of the various flowers adorning the octagonal wedding arch under which I, my betrothed, and our officiant stood were truly something to behold. My gaze was more on them than my partner throughout the ceremony.

Not that my beloved wasn't a sight to behold in his dapper suit, so sleek and black, making him seem like he had been carved from a beautiful midnight sky. His eyes, encroaching stars, destined (given the chance) to become suns pulling others into his orbit as he'd pulled me.

At that point, I was the one. Had confidence that I would stay the one. Then and forever. Those eyes would never get the chance to roam and attract others. As I had worked on myself, I would maintain myself, distracting any and all who might feel they had a chance at allowing my man to bestow upon them even a fraction of his essence.

I—the blushing bride—would stay at his side, and I'd be sure to outshine at all times. Just as I stood with him under our arch, undoubtedly outshining, bedecked in a two-piece ivory gown. Sheath silhouette. Satin. Densely woven silk. *Lustrous.*

I was enveloped, it seemed, in an abundance of silk. Some of it pressed tightly against my skin, while other layers flowed loosely about my body, caught up in the playful breezes. At times during the ceremony, I must have seemed engulfed in white fire.

My body was toned. My skin, perfect, of course. Perfect for one's most perfect of days. Blemish-free. *Glowing.* My head was clear. No traumatic-memory lightning strikes. My therapists had done their job. I was all smiles.

Until my face, my head, my body could no longer bear the weight. The burden of lies. The heft of dangerous falsehoods.

It wasn't supposed to be like this. Was never supposed to be like this, like what had occurred. After I'd risen from the dead, my new life should at some point have been guided onto a rising path, one that placed me among the roses. Blossoms of every shade and hue, maybe even a few as yet unseen or unheard of. *No need to pick any; they had picked me.*

All those metaphorical roses, the unambiguous signs of a woman who'd made it, who had it *all*. A fun and lucrative and enriching career. Two or three bright, cheerful, and all-around wonderful children. A gorgeous husband who both complemented me and complimented me, who didn't complain, who never bored me with anything nearing repetition.

But the path hadn't risen; it only seemed to as it wound and threaded, leading me this way and that, inclining and declining, through parks and meadows and woodlands, making me forget that everything had its necessary flaws.

None of what adorned the arch were roses. It was just a colorful, aromatic, and intertwined mass of toxic weeds. *Pick your poison . . .*

There were no perfect lives. There were no perfect children. No perfect careers. No perfect partners—as mine had reminded me at the reception. Shortly after we'd cut the cake.

That had been when the burden of smiling became too great.

We'd opted for a casual cocktail-style reception. Outside,

amid lush greenery, with evenly spaced lounge areas; high-top cocktail tables for standing and drinking; lower, wider round tables for sitting and eating, not to mention the various food stations and open bar. Alcohol and conversations flowed freely while half a dozen of the caterer's gloved and uniformed staff threaded through it all, gliding from guest to guest, offering selections from their plates of hors d'oeuvres.

After cutting the cake, we didn't smear the sweetness on each other's faces. We did feed each other. Just one forkful. Just for show. Once the guests got on with enjoying their cake slices, I thought I'd finish mine—only to hear a low growl from my husband, followed by him muttering, "Careful . . ."

I'd turned to him, my eyebrows raised. "What?"

"You need to be careful with sugar. You know how you are, what can happen to your body."

My eyes had narrowed at that point. "And just how am I? What exactly can happen?"

"Nothing. Just forget it."

"How can I just forget it? You're obviously trying to remind me of something. Some flaw in me. My *being*."

He'd sighed. Ostentatiously. "I'm just saying overly sweet foods . . . They can go to your head."

"My head? And my thighs, too, maybe? Is that what you're worried about? A fat and manic wife?"

"See. This is why I said forget it."

"You also said that I know how I am. But your statement implied my state of blissful ignorance. So you were obviously trying to enlighten me. So what about it, headshrinker? Mister Thought Massager?"

He'd gone back to muttering to himself, looking away. But by now, we'd drawn the attention of others. We'd elicited their sneers. Derisive laughter. From three of them in particular.

Their faces were grotesque. Their eyes, glowing like

embers. Soon everyone looked like these three. The appearance, demeanor, hostile hilarity—all of it was infectious among our guests, whose glowing eyes were on me. Their gazes, penetrating.

I removed mine from them, from my husband. Left my chin lowered.

I wasn't looking forward to the first dance with my new husband. But I looked at the plate before me, focused on the cake.

Perfection wasn't in life. Certainly not in my life. But in the cake . . .

Crystals. All the sugar crystals that had gone into making the cake, the frosting, the rest of it, all the layers upon layers. How many had dissolved during some part of the process? How many remain crystallized? *Deeper.* My sight drilled down to the depths—microscoping, ultrafocusing, deeper and deeper—until I saw them, individuated them . . . a trove of crystals.

My body quivered as the cake disintegrated into a mass of dancing particles: shivering white crystals embodying light, moving farther and farther away from one another. At a certain distance, the light within each acquired a hue; each crystal took on one of many colors that pulsed. To its own unique beat, each crystal emitted rays in a variety of directions. Each ray connected with some of the others, establishing a pulsing web of light and leaving the crystals as nodules—multifaceted beads that possessed more than light.

As I focused on one, then another, I realized the crystals harbored images, moving pictures, multidimensional scenes of which I was a part. I saw snippets of past slights, humiliations, public degradations. I also saw possibilities, things that hadn't happened, but could have. Maybe should have. Scenes of me exacting revenge.

But the more nodules I focused on, the more I saw other

individuals featured, each in their own foul situations and executing their own unique payback against those who'd wronged them. These others, they were the same women and men who'd been with me in the bar. The same ones who'd died with me. The ones who'd been resurrected with me—many of them destined to die again at their own hands.

What did it mean? What did it mean I was seeing their imagined scenarios?

Just forget it. Never mind.

I was escaping from a wedding. A sweet-turned-sour ceremony portending a foul life bound to another with the leechlike ligatures of false love.

I was escaping through these sugar crystals, giving myself over to their web, acknowledging that the diamonds—the crystalline flowers—on my new ring were treacherous, understanding that my body no longer belonged wholly to myself. My life—my *reborn* life, if I willingly continued on the path I belatedly realized someone else had paved, would continue deeper into gloom and, ultimately, doom.

I sought the light. I actively sought the multifaceted nodule —the crystal—harboring the image of me experiencing the slight, the degradation, the humiliation of being reborn. And I sought the scenario of revenge.

As I searched through this cake, frantically, at the deepest level, I felt the crystals permeating my body. I felt them sprouting hinged limbs and scuttling throughout my being as I experienced multiple scenarios at once, vivid images, all blurring together, bathing my vision in a yellowish light that increasingly paled, then shut off.

I found myself in darkness. Floating. Undulating in black space.

Intuition told me I had gone back, too far back. Seeking the circumstances of my rebirth, I had instead placed myself in my mother's womb.

But how was that possible?

I was conscious. I was aware of having some form, some kind of body, but that was it. I had no sensation. I picked up no sounds.

Then I heard a loud tone, like the short ring of a doorbell, followed by two more. Shortly after, a dull light crept from the periphery, gradually brightening my surroundings.

I had, indeed, been floating. I, indeed, had a body, naked as the day I was born. I was even inside a womb-like device—but it certainly didn't belong to my mother.

My mind fully returned to the here and now, full awareness of myself and surroundings, as my eyes met a white ceiling, curved, concave, only a couple of feet from my face. Under and around me, the water began to churn. It was only then that I felt it, recognized the water as being separate from my body, though part of me wondered if it and my body had truly been homogenous while I was out.

I turned to my right and reached for the handle, using it to steady myself as I repositioned from floating on my back to kneeling in salt water about two feet deep. I paused to take a deep breath before lifting the handle, rising to my feet as I opened the hatch all the way.

Sensing movement, the surrounding room's lights switched on. Before stepping out of the pod, my eyes flashed to right, toward the racks and hooks where I'd left my clothes. Adjacent to them were stacks of neatly folded towels and washcloths.

Carefully, I stepped out of the pod, out of the churning waters and onto the tile floor, trying my best not to slosh or otherwise bring much of the salt water with me.

I gingerly made my way to the towels, grabbed two of them and one washcloth, then retraced some of my steps, passing by the self-cleaning pod on toward the wooden bench. I dropped the towels on the bench and, washcloth in hand, continued toward the shower in the corner of the room.

Flotation therapy. Sensory deprivation. It benefited the minds of its participants, particularly those who did it frequently, like at least once a week. But the benefits those others received differed from what was given to me. The therapy wasn't just massaging my mind. It was manipulating my subconscious. Perhaps the deepest layers of my body as well.

No—there was no "perhaps" to it. I knew it was doing something to my body. Something in addition to all the other adjustments that had been made to it over the years. I just didn't know exactly what it was. All I knew was that I no longer knew myself. Not completely. A belated realization. Something I should have begun to suspect eight years ago, after I died in the bar.

Back then, after regaining life in the field, I hadn't paid an excessive amount of attention to my body. I knew it was different, but what differences I'd felt and noticed I'd chalked up to having essentially been blanked out of existence for a few months. But over time, my body continued to change, develop. I incrementally grew taller, a centimeter or two every few months, a process so gradual I didn't notice until I was several inches taller than I should have been.

Posture had been a factor.

As I had throughout my life, I worked out on rainy days or during periods when I was bored or when I remembered my physician had said it was a good idea or when girlfriends dragged me along to whatever fad workout spot they were all hyped up about. But I was never a nut about it. The further I lived on from my rebirth, the more I felt the need to make exercise a regular habit. My body urged me—practically forced me

—to work out at regular intervals. Where once before I might have found myself pouring a glass of Chablis after a long day of working at the firm, post-rebirth I would find myself falling like a plank to the floor to do a few sets of push-ups.

Cycling, jogging, weights—I did what I could fit into my schedule. I did what exercises my muscles urged me to do. Of course, such workouts left me physically drained, and whenever I had to walk anywhere, it showed.

Sometimes I would walk with my shoulders slumped or with my shoulders leading, ever in danger of the slightest trip sending me to fall down flat on my face. Other times, it would be a sloppy amble, as if my legs wanted to go every direction but forward. And there were times when I just shuffled, sleepily, invisible brooms behind my feet the only things pushing me along.

Those days, I never strutted or strode with confidence. With an erect posture. I didn't carry myself like the ethereal being I eventually realized I had become.

When I made the conscious decision to have my diet match my workouts, I had more energy. More energy encouraged, and I expanded my range of workouts to climbing, longer-distance running at a faster pace on bumpy trails and through obstacle-heavy woods, heavier weights, kickboxing . . . But it was only after I began yoga that I noticed how much my body had changed. How much I'd grown. In so many ways.

The water from the shower's nozzle pelted me like lukewarm lightning strikes. Here at the spa, the showers were programmed to go through a range. Soft-flowing at first, encouraging the one under the water to douse herself. After a couple of minutes, the flow strengthened, encouraging the one under the water to move on to the next step—lathering herself, perhaps.

I'd taken a shower prior to stepping into the flotation pod.

Standard procedure. One needed to wash all lotions, hair conditioners, oils, and whatever other contaminating substances from the surface of the body to ensure a good and proper float. Afterward, one needed to wash the salt from their hair and skin. But I had embedded flecks I couldn't wash off or even pick out.

After drying myself thoroughly, I made my way to the stool and counter next to where my new clothes hung. Choosing from among the selection of specially made beauty products, I applied the prescribed lotions, hair care products, and all the other stuff that would help beautify and preserve my vessel—a body housing a soul that was no longer whole. A small but significant piece of it belonged to the witch.

I made myself up the way she had demanded, only glancing at the mirror until it was time to pretty up my face and hair. This required a more sustained gaze. I couldn't avoid the embedded flecks in my skin. Flakes of flawed gems.

Spaced an inch or so apart, they were like translucent quartz—at least to my casual eyes. To most observers, they were invisible unless vibrating, the light from outside my body hitting my skin just right while the internal processes began a fight or flight or another response to the situation that had put me on my guard.

An intimate part of my physical body with a direct channel to my incomplete soul, the crystals assisted with the manipulation of light particles, a process that occurred both consciously and sub. Sometime by intuition, sometimes by reflex. Entangling electromagnetic radiation from outside my body with what I retained of my soul—the essence of my consciousness—I could work wonders.

Some of the feats I wondered about more than others.

I could use the crystals to help me manipulate not only what is commonly known as light but also, at will, what I retained of my own soul. Dehydrating and hydrating myself. Sending the essence of my consciousness to another dimension. Shifting and moving myself from place to place, on various levels of Reality.

I had only a vague awareness of what actually occurred to the physical part of me during this process: the body shrank and dehydrated, and biological functions were suspended. For all I knew (and what I strongly suspected), the entire vessel was temporarily dispersed into a mass of loosely connected dust particles entangled with particles of light and preserved by—maybe even attached to or subsumed within—the crystalline flecks. Whatever, it endured extreme environmental conditions while waiting, even teleporting to another place until I was ready to reassemble, synchronizing my soul's frequency with that mass of dust, remaking it into clay, re-forming my body, healing it if and when necessary from whatever it may have endured while the essence of my consciousness was otherwise occupied.

I didn't need the flotation pod, but using the witch's device was a way for her to maintain some level of control over the process so that I didn't stray too far—her possession of a piece of my soul notwithstanding.

Shortly after placing myself in the pod, lying still in a supine position, I'd absorbed and manipulated the pod ceiling's light that showered the front of my body. As the light gradually dimmed, the pod deprived me of my common senses, allowing me to concentrate enough to do what I needed to.

And I'd failed her. Again.

Now I had to make myself presentable for my report.

No mere spa robe would do. Not even a high-end one. It was insisted that I dress in the clothes provided. A navy-blue suit—single-button jacket, A-line skirt—and heels. The same sort of outfit I might have worn at the office if I'd still been a practicing attorney. No idea why, other than it probably amused her in some fashion. A reminder that I now worked for her. That I was essentially bought and paid for.

Fully garbed, I unlocked and slid open the door to view a dim, empty corridor and the green door at the far end.

Mindful of my posture, I trod carefully as I passed by the closed doors on either side, some of them harboring other women or men going through their own unique therapies and treatments. I lent none of them much thought. I concentrated on making my entrance, immediately appearing to those on the other side of the green door as one worthy of my semi-divine status.

At about ten paces away from the verdant portal, I paused to take a deep breath.

Releasing it, feeling ready, I proceeded. The door slid open automatically when I was within five paces.

Directly in front of me, a few dozen steps away in a cushioned rattan peacock chair, sat the witch. Her right hand rested in her lap; her left held aloft a tulip shaped glass half-full of a ruddy liquid—undoubtedly Cabernet. She was flanked by six other people. Four women and two men. An equal number on either side. All six wore high-end workout gear—hot pink, blazing blue, and unsettled silver—the apparel one might find on young trophy wives and toy-prize husbands who had the time to work out, hang out, and shop all day, all while wearing the same outfit. In truth, they were all college-aged kids. In great shape, sure, but firmly hooked on the pharmaceuticals Carmilla provided and deeply enthralled by her less-tangible charms.

Stunningly beautiful people, the entire sextet. The witch, however, was on her own level.

Just on the cusp of leaving her teens, the oddly tanned girl wore black stretch trousers, white stiletto boots, and an ash-gray wrap scarf sweater that hardly covered her matching one-shoulder bralette. Ears and neck, fingers and wrists, and even her exposed ankles displayed an abundance of gems and jewelry—all sparkling, twinkling, and gleaming. I knew there was even more underneath the trappings of her clothing. Carmilla was a stuffed jewelry box turned into flesh then turned inside out.

The door whooshed shut behind me as I stepped forward, stopping when the witch-girl raised her right hand, showing me her palm.

With the same hand, she gestured toward the water cooler on a nearby shelf, nestled between a stack of paper cups and a potted peace lily. "Have some."

"No thank you." No telling what mind- or body-altering substances laced the clear liquid. "I'm not thirsty." Though I was. The pod's salt water had left me feeling dehydrated.

I controlled my facial expression. My hoarse voice, however, probably gave me away. Carmilla's brow knit together.

"Drink," she repeated. "It has notes of lemon."

Wondering for what "lemon" might be a euphemism, I drifted toward the cooler. Upon reaching it, I didn't—couldn't—hesitate to lift a paper cup and fill it. I also couldn't help but feel everyone's eyes on me as I did.

Imbibing, I detected notes of lime, not lemon, and wondered whether I should say anything.

Why had Carmilla commented about the taste? I mean *really*? Was I supposed to notice the difference and speak up? If I spoke up, would she be impressed by my noting the distinction? Or would she be insulted I had dared contradiction? And what was the citrus masking anyway? If anything?

All these questions . . . She was in my head. Of course she

was. Screwing with me. That was the point. She delighted in her subtle ways of constantly reminding me.

I helped myself to a second cup of water, then turned back toward her with a faint smile on my lips, conveying I'd been happily refreshed. I resolved to say nothing unless asked.

Her brow remained furrowed. "Well?"

"I—" My words caught in my throat.

"*Did* you find him? *Do* you know where he is?"

"I . . . I think I'm getting closer."

"What the hell does that mean?"

"I believe he's at a wedding."

"*What?*"

When her right hand flew to the chair's arm, I thought she was going to leap forward. Maybe go for my throat, clawing at it. Or maybe smash the wine glass against my cheek. But she remained seated, her right-hand fingers clutching the chair's arm like talons.

"I was at a wedding," I said. "My own, but very different. And . . . I felt his presence."

Carmilla's eyes narrowed, penetrating. She didn't take them off me even when sipping. The eyes of the other six drilled into me as well. I remained calm, unflinching.

The witch swallowed then spoke through gritted teeth, slowly. "Your task is very simple. Find where the doctor is hiding. Or discover the formula needed to wake up our sleeping beauty—permanently."

Yeah—very simple. The formula would be a mix of ritual, incantation, and medicines. The witch wanted not only a list, a recitation of details, but also explicit instructions on how to put all the components to use.

"Now," Carmilla said. "You've made no mention of a formula. You show no signs of possessing one. But what you are telling me is that you still, after all you've been through, you *still* have no idea where Doctor Jim Linkins is. You just *felt* a presence."

She sneered before taking another sip of wine. She closed her eyes as she swallowed, muttered something under her breath.

Her eyes slowly opened as she said, "If Linkins is willfully hiding, I can understand, to an extent, how he eludes you. But after all the training, after everything I've given and allowed you, how, at this point, have you not been able to extract from your experiences the formula we need?"

I swallowed, looked her dead in her eyes, maintained my posture. "You've taught me well. But I am not as talented as you. Mistress."

The flattery, capped off with the designation she preferred from her loyal acolytes, was an attempt to soften her. I wasn't sure it had worked.

She rose from her seat, handed her glass to the nearest acolyte on her left, and stepped a few paces toward me, all the while holding my gaze. She said nothing. Roughly six paces in front of me, she stopped, gradually lowered her eyes, running them over my person.

Maybe she felt I was wasting her time. Maybe she was considering punishments. Or maybe she was thinking deeply about what I'd said while also attempting to read the crystals in my exposed skin.

The crystals worked for me, but they could also work well for one of her talents.

They, in part, worked off the power of my memories—those powerful lights within me. Significant components of my soul. Memories fueled the crystals as much as the various wavelengths of light hitting my skin. Of course, my nervous system and semi-divine blood were also factors; they did their part in powering the crystals.

But my memories . . . If Carmilla was searching me now, it was because of those. After all, according to her, it was Doctor Linkins himself who had walked into the bar all those years ago. He was the man responsible for what had happened that night. I did not remember his face. With a portion of my soul—a small piece of the essence of my consciousness—inaccessible to me, many of my memories were as well.

This doctor, he had done all sorts of things to my ability to remember important bits about myself. He was the one who had taken a bit of my soul, a bit that somehow had eventually found its way into Carmilla's possession. But he'd done even more to me. Made me a puzzle to myself. And to Carmilla.

Beyond the complete control or domination of either of them, I knew enough to know that I had been blessed. Been given more than a hint of divinity. Hence, my abilities. Hence, the reason Linkins had come at me in the first place. Hence, why he tried to do a number on me.

But I was limited in what I could do. How far I could go. What I could accomplish. In part because of Linkins and in part because of Carmilla. He wanted to keep me away from him. She wanted to keep me until she found him—him or his wake-up formula. I wanted to be free of them and forget them both. For all three of us, my memories were the key.

Presently, some of the memories I retained were playing with the crystals. All over my body, they vibrated—though only my face and hands and lower portion of my legs were on display to the witch. Carmilla running her eyes over me had triggered the internal processes that would soon result in fight, flight, or another response.

In an attempt to prevent any of the above—anything but standing straight and stone faced—my gaze fell from Carmilla's eyes to her mouth. Her lips were pressed tightly together. But she wasn't frowning. She wasn't grinding her teeth.

Soon she exhaled a long breath through her nose. Internally, I pushed myself to relax further and was careful to not let my posture show it. I actually had softened her. Enough for her to reconsider what I'd said about a wedding.

Twinkle, twinkle—every flawed gem . . .

The witch dealt in symbolism. What I'd told her, just that little bit—she knew it meant something, possibly something grand. She was trying to read the bits and pieces of my memories that her arts allowed her to access, turn everything over in her head, and come up with possibilities before she deigned to ask me what I thought.

"Give me details," she said suddenly, her eyes meeting mine. "Everything. Setting. Words spoken. Number of guests. Attire. *Everything.*"

I told her everything I recalled, down to the minutest detail. Everything I could pull to the surface of my consciousness.

Carmilla listened intently, taking mental notes. Her eyes widened as I discussed my impression of my groom's appearance; her jaw did the same when I discussed the three grotesque faces, the mockers who infected all the others.

When I finished, her mouth closed. Her chin lowered as she contemplated. It raised suddenly as she began to ask me a question, but her words were interrupted by another's one.

"Mistress."

A dark-haired woman with a gaunt face had poked her head through the beaded curtain to my left, Carmilla's right. Gateway to another corridor that led to another section of the spa.

Carmilla fluttered her right hand at the woman. "Not now."

"It is important."

"So is this."

"The *girl*," the dark-haired woman bellowed, drawing all eyes in the room to her. "She's *up*. And singing."

Carmilla's eyebrows arched as she gaped at the messenger.

Briefly returning her attention to me, her eyes narrowed as she stabbed her index finger toward my nose. "I'm not finished with you yet. Wait here."

Carmilla turned and brisked through the beaded curtain, following the woman who spoke now in a rushed yet hushed voice. I was only able to determine that some sort of breakthrough had occurred. The semi-vegetative girl had awakened before, after all. But the singing . . . Was that new?

I recalled that when we woke up in the field all those years ago, we each awoke to a sung phrase, a snippet of a song. What had that meant? What did this, happening now, mean?

As I mulled possibilities, my gaze fell to the floor; it gradually rose again when I felt the six others staring ice daggers at me.

My eyes met each of theirs in turn. All of them scowled, their irises glowing bright blue or yellowish green or dark red from behind narrowed lids.

I didn't know them. Not individually. But I knew all about them.

They were from the would-be professional class. Destined to become white-shoe lawyers, top-shelf investment managers, physicians and dentists to the rich.

Owing to family connections—to say nothing of family money—they'd been able to get into top schools. Schools for which their brains had been ill equipped. They weren't unique among that type. Many well-heeled kids made it into schools that were beyond their intellectual capacity but somehow—by hook or crook, by greasing wheels, by papering palms—managed to coast through.

These six before me, however, had probably really wanted

to do well. They had wanted the good grades and the professorial accolades that would help them attain their desired profession, their deserved position in the wider world of racing rats and heavyset cats. So they'd had to study harder than ever before. To do so, they'd needed some studying aids, the kind of aids one could only procure on the black market.

And that's where the wretched little witch had come in.

The spoiled daughter of hotshot drug developers, Carmilla found her connects and exploited them early in her life, well before her teen years, all while studying the deviant arts of magick. As the nasty, naughty, and spiritually lit Lolita got older, developed her network, she peddled experimental drugs to the highest willing bidders, all of them inevitably older than she was. High-achieving college and grad students were among her customers.

I was among her customers. Unknowingly.

Law school had been difficult. With the changes in my body and the accompanying psychological stress, I couldn't completely focus. Couldn't get much done without some assistance. A chemical savior. Or two.

When I reached out for help, a friend of a friend (who was also a classmate—a unique one who was not competitive) connected me with a friend of an associate of Carmilla's. What she was peddling helped me get through law school. Acquiring my supply from a third party, I knew nothing of the witch. Not until I was "called."

My experience in the bar that night and the aftermath . . .

The poison of her medicinals running through my system

. . .

Freshly graduated from law school and newly ensconced in a respectable firm, I was well on the road to becoming completely lost to myself. With Carmilla's special blend of chemicals running through my veins, it was nothing for her to use her magick to curve that road and have it wind toward her—or, more specifically, toward a wine bar that she'd rented out for an afternoon.

Me and others in a similar station were her audience. Cracked but not yet fully broken beings. Ambitious vessels.

Almost all of us were older than she was. A good percentage of us were women. I discovered later an even better percentage of attendees not only had Carmilla's poisons running through them but also harbored a strange virus, one that endowed its possessors with many fantastic abilities, including the ability to manipulate light.

The wine meeting was one of dozens—scores, maybe even hundreds—that Carmilla had had with several groups. Each such gathering kicked into high gear the grooming process that had begun with exotic, off-market drugs. In the flesh-and-bone cauldrons of those who would be her acolytes, she used her words and other charms to stir chemicals, saturating their minds, likely cackling mentally to herself all the while.

Unlike the others who bowed, I remained resistant. The crystals in my flesh were a big part of the reason. They also made me more valuable to the witch than her increasingly physically powerful yet increasingly mindless goons.

These six before me—glaring, their eyes glowing—they had at some point gotten their final call from Carmilla. They were now lost to their families. Written off as deceased in many cases. They'd new names and new purposes in their controlled lives.

Their eyes literally shined but were dead. There was no true spark. Carmilla possessed and controlled the entirety or a majority of their souls. She was their owner. Keeper. Their enslaver.

Damn her and her therapies. Carmilla had a bit of my soul; I couldn't let her have even a sliver more. Yet she'd tried. And would keep trying. The witch had set up shops within my mental real estate. I knew how to evade them; when and how to patronize them; and, so far, how to prevent them from expanding their territory in my mind. That wouldn't last forever.

Carmilla parted the beaded curtain with her hands.

"*You*."

From a longer distance this time, she stabbed her finger toward my nose.

"Come with me."

She didn't wait for me to move before she took a step backward and turned, heading back down the corridor. Pea-size baubles clacked against one another as the hanging strings swayed left and right, easing toward silent verticality.

I glanced once more at the wordless six before heading for the curtain, stirring up the beads again as I pushed through. Quickening my pace, I trailed three steps behind Carmilla down a winding corridor of sand-hued walls and tiger's-eye doors. My heart leaped in my chest when we turned suddenly into a blindingly white, antiseptic corridor. It put me in the mind of a hospital. Or a laboratory.

As was appropriate.

I followed Carmilla through another curtain—black, silky—into another room. A five-walled room. I guessed that, normally, the sun's rays filtered down through the skylight above when the sky permitted the sun to shine. Prior to beginning my therapy for the day, the forecast had called for rain. I heard no patter of drops on glass, but the skylight allowed wan light from an overcast sky to enter this enclosure, where a complex process of light therapy was taking place.

A variety of lamps had been situated around the room, in a pattern I couldn't discern but knew existed based on the witch's habits, her twitchy ways. Some hung from the ceiling; some jutted from one of the five walls; others were floor lamps. All had bases that seemed a maze of thin pipes, a mass of criss-crossing fibers, or some other byzantine design. Grids. Maps. Circulatory systems. Masses of tendrils and roots, wires and nerves.

The complicated structures' bulbs emitted a range from across the electromagnetic spectrum, a variety of light and colors—some pulsing in rhythm, some flowing in a steady stream, some periodically flooding the area, others flashing in an esoteric code. The rays from all lamps eventually hit and filtered through the coffin's glass, passing through to kiss, wash, or bathe the naked body of the redheaded girl inside.

Marie-Lydia McGillis. A plump and pale young teenager constellated with freckles, old scars, and fresh bruises. To the casual onlooker, she would appear to be at peace. The ultimate peace.

Adjusting my vision, I could see the web of lights of which she was the center; many of the web's components were beyond the range of a human's immediate senses. And the girl, she was certainly *beyond.*

Neither fully alive nor fully dead, the girl was in a semi-vegetative state. Mostly sleeping—deeply—but occasionally, she would awaken, open and step out of her pod, and even talk. But she wouldn't respond to external prompting. One could not engage her in conversation. If she looked at you, there was no indication she could see you, let alone react to anything you might do to her or in front of her.

She was kept housed—safe—in the translucent pod, which, to my eyes, resembled a crystalline coffin, though Carmilla didn't refer to it as such. Whichever, it sustained her body, harnessing a range of light that nourished the millions of para-sites living within her skin and blood.

The girl was a victim of both the White Fire Virus and an

assault by another girl who'd possessed the same miraculous malady.

Carmilla shared significant responsibility for the girl's present condition. No telling what the witch had planned for her once she regained full mobility and consciousness.

"I only caught the end of her performance," Carmilla said. "Rather suddenly, she had to be placed back into her chamber. But what I caught and what Marta was able to tell me were illuminating."

I didn't ask if she was willing to share. Certainly didn't expect her to. So it was a bit of a shock to see Carmilla fiddle with her phone and say, "I want you to witness something" before thrusting the phone, screen forward, toward my face.

Carmilla had recorded what little she'd seen and, presently, I watched.

The redheaded girl was free of her coffin, levitating, slow dancing with herself in a swirl of blue and red and green and violet lights while dolefully reciting lyrics, a portion of a verse.

> . . . tainted blood, haunted silk.
> Fire, white—born red ice.
> Sun is death. Moon is life.
> Bonded two, groom and wife—

The girl then collapsed and was deftly caught by the dark-haired, gaunt-faced woman, Marta, who prevented a nasty fall. As skillfully as if she'd done it dozens of times by now, Marta carried the girl and gently placed her back into her glass coffin.

Marta moved with grace, like a trained dancer. But while my eyes followed the action, my thoughts dwelled. *Those words.*

Ordinarily, I would say they had the makings of the worst

poem I'd ever heard. But, of course, I didn't say it. I even tried to erase any trace of criticism from my head.

Carmilla lowered her phone, slid it into her pocket.

Maintaining proper posture, I kept a stony expression—didn't wince or raise an eyebrow, even as I noticed Carmilla gazing at my forehead.

"It seems you made some progress after all," she said in a honeyed voice. "Marta filled me in on what I'd missed, but for your purposes, it's not important."

Yeah—Carmilla was done sharing.

"But it appears we are nearly done. Our relationship at its end." She smiled broadly at me with tightly pressed lips, an expression I couldn't readily decipher. "I need an evening to meditate on all this, but rest assured, tomorrow will be a big day. For you. For us."

I kept my face blank.

"I will have a mission for you," she continued. "You succeed, and, well, I will gift you the piece of your soul that fell into my possession. You will no longer be in my debt."

A mission. I knew before I even heard any details that it would be planned based on something I'd done, something I'd dredged up, something I unburied sufficiently to allow the witch to see and study it. Carmilla acted as if she were doing me a favor by offering me this; but without me, she wouldn't even have a plan. Still, I smiled graciously as I looked her in the eye.

"What would you have me do in the meantime, Mistress?"

Carmilla glanced at Marta, giving her a quick nod. Marta turned on her heel and exited through the black curtain.

"You'll be put up for the night. Await further instructions. Janice will show you to your accommodations."

"Where?" It was impertinent to ask, but I couldn't help it.

Carmilla cocked her head slightly to the left and smiled

deviously. "Someplace special. First thing in the morning, you are to go and make confession." She ran her eyes over me slowly, lasciviously. "You'll need it."

A woman with a layered blonde pixie bob entered the room through the black curtain. She wore tight blue jeans and a loose, long-sleeved, grayish-green tunic top. Janice, I presumed.

Carmilla only glanced at the woman before returning to me. "I paid a pretty penny for you, Jenny. For your temporary services. And I fully expect you'll do what's required, ensure that I get my money's worth."

However she'd acquired the fraction of my soul, it hadn't been cheap—a point she'd made before. Maybe saying it one more time was her way of bidding me adieu.

She gestured toward the blonde, who, in turn, beckoned with two fingers for me to follow her out through the black curtain. I did so without a word, without another glance at Carmilla, who I could feel smirking behind me as I trailed the pseudonymous "Janice" down the blinding white corridor into passageways easier on my eyes.

Her name was no more Janice than mine was Jenny, but Carmilla had branded me with a moniker. One she chose and preferred. She had branded this other woman with a similar name, a name-for-the-moment that could and would give her influence over me. Keep me in line.

The woman walked like a classically trained dancer, as gracefully as many of Carmilla's followers, despite the fact she was wearing stiletto boots. Just under six feet tall without the footwear, the woman was in her late twenties or early thirties and undoubtedly adept in one or two martial arts and just as many manners of street brawling. She was a Spryte—one of the witch's acolytes who could manipulate electromagnetic radiation and her body in almost unbelievable ways. The six who'd accompanied Carmilla and the others receiving treatments in the spa were all in training, aspiring to reach the status of Spryte, if not something greater.

After another turn into a short hallway, Janice pushed open an exit door. We stepped into cool afternoon air onto a white concrete pathway that led to the parking lot.

Gleaming sports cars lay before us, a dozen of them, situated like the black squares on a checkerboard. The relatively smooth blacktop retained few puddles, shallow ones that wouldn't sully the sides of anyone's shoes. Janice led me toward a silver vehicle.

A Jaguar XKR coupe. Convertible. Top of the line. And modified. Leftover rainwater decorated its exterior with translucent pearls.

Carmilla wasn't necessarily uber rich, but she had connections. And once she decided she desired something, she could be very persuasive in the process of obtaining, whether she did so directly or through another party. Those gems, those crystals, all that jewelry adorning her person—they channeled a hell of a lot of power.

When Janice pushed the button on her keys to unlock the vehicle, I glanced at her, half expecting that she'd want me to hold the driver's door open for her.

But in one smooth motion, she opened her own door, slid behind the wheel, and started the car. With somewhat less grace, I settled in the passenger's seat and fastened my seat belt, triple-checking that it was truly locked.

I checked twice more as Janice sped the Jaguar down slickened streets, weaving back and forth between lanes.

The afternoon shower had come and gone, but a light fog remained. The woman didn't bother with lights or wipers. Like mine, her eyes could cut through all of it just fine. And she handled the vehicle like it was simply the lower half of her own agile body.

As for any cop who might dare to pull us over . . . Well, I was no mind reader, but I could tell she was wanting it. Itching to use one of a variety of tricks to outfox the badges. Using her abilities to turn the car invisible. Testing other talents that would enable her to outmaneuver and outrun them. Or just letting them pull her over and using her eyes and voice to hypnotize, maybe even get them to pull their guns and blow their own brains out.

Carmilla's acolytes were a thrill-seeking and sadistic bunch. I wondered exactly how I had been before I'd gotten mixed up with her.

Jenny wasn't my original name, but damned if I could remember what was. I did know that a female donkey was known as a jenny. A male donkey, a jack. A donkey in general was related to a mule. Like a carrier mule. A celestial mule. One harboring seeds for a new world. Jenny—a pretty nick-name. Short for the ugly idea of genocide.

I closed my eyes, swallowed. Musing too much on my given name inevitably took me—as fast and as recklessly as Janice was driving—to dark psychological spaces where I didn't want to dwell.

My real name, I did not know. With my abilities, however, I was quite familiar. And while in the service of the witch, I had a sole purpose: to locate or obtain the esoteric knowledge of Jim "Jimmy" Linkins. Doctor by profession. Metaphysician of God by self-description, according to the witch-girl Carmilla. In her eyes, Linkins was the enemy. Her archenemy. But she needed his assistance in reviving a living-dead girl, one whom Carmilla had made her pet project.

With her quest for this doctor, Carmilla had come as close as she ever would to admitting that she, using her own knowl-edge and talents, couldn't awaken the girl—not permanently. She would never say it, but it was no secret. And it wasn't necessarily a knock against her dark arts and crafts. It was primarily the doctor's fault the girl had ended up in her condition in the first place. He likely knew a trick or two that would help her recover.

He likely knew a trick or two that would help free me from Carmilla's thrall as well.

After all, he was the one who began the process of my death and rebirth. A devil, perhaps doing the work of angels unwittingly. Or maybe just a scheming evildoer interfering with God's intentions.

As time passed after my rebirth, not only did my body change, but my eyes also gradually opened to the fact that there weren't just ordinary men and women on this planet. There were other classes of beings, other realms of Reality.

Those others who'd woken up with me in the field—they, like me, had been destined to become something. Something similar or different but surely divinely gifted. We all had been tortured and extinguished, only to be recycled, reborn. We were all given new bodies (even if we didn't realize it at the time), new chances (even if we didn't understand it at the time), new paths to achieving something great (even though those routes were, at that time, obscured). Time was what all of us needed to realize our potential. Time and therapies. But time wasn't on the side of the others. Something had gone wrong with their minds. Wrong with their bodies. Or their souls just couldn't take the weight. So they were extinguished a second time: this time, by their own hands.

Back then, there were times I wondered whether it would have been wise for me to condemn myself to the same fate. But, through therapy, I came to realize I'd been Providence-kised. I came to understand that I'd been chosen—*we'd* been chosen— to become higher beings, to perform divine work on Earth, to access other realms of Reality in order to perform our sacred duties.

But there was also a devil. There were others in his orbit. And there was a witch.

And there was me, with my purpose. My most immediate purpose. Whether I'd subconsciously searched for and found it or it had been made my reason for my being—my being where I was and what I was at this moment in time—I willingly accepted it.

Save the girl.

The witch Carmilla made it clear that, as far as she was concerned, my most immediate purpose was to either find where Doctor Linkins was hiding or discover the formula needed to wake up the girl.

My goals for my new life were to release the girl from her current state and set her free, truly free, and then take back my own independence, clear of Carmilla and her ilk. Deep down, I knew that somehow, attaining this second goal would require me to discover what I'd never found—a true love of myself.

Like copulating snakes, the witch's interests and mine intertwined and deviated. Possessing a piece of my soul gave her an upper hand, but I was determined to cut that hand off before she truly got the better of me.

And I was determined to cut off Carmilla's connection with the girl. It wasn't only because of her age. The girl was certainly no innocent babe. She had attacked her high school classmates. Killed dozens. Hurt many more.

Though some in high places had managed to convince most of the population that the whole scenario had been an elaborate hoax (paying off families and witnesses and disappearing those too rockheaded to take the bribes), I knew all too well the tragedy was true. I'd seen the videos. I recognized that the girl exhibiting supernatural abilities and exacting punishments on her peers was one who possessed the White Fire Virus, an infernal disease that poisoned bodies and minds, making the infected feel and believe and act as if they were truly chosen, truly divine, truly blessed—as I had been blessed and chosen.

The girl had been confused, troubled, dangerous. So when she assaulted her fellow students, teachers, and school administrators with dazzling lights and lasers and vicious holograms, I knew it wasn't just the elaborate art project the Heartland Security Agency and some of their friends in the media had claimed it was.

Marie-Lydia McGillis. Still living, her entire soul was already damned, trapped in a hellish realm beyond my access. A would-be acolyte of Carmilla's. I figured the witch had nefarious ambitions for her, but I sensed the girl could resist the witch, just as I could resist her. Marie-Lydia would prove to be too strong for Carmilla's charms. But Marie-Lydia had to wake up first. I had to help her wake up.

Carmilla's other, older acolytes—they were too far gone. Nothing could be done for them. Drugs had ravaged their minds, making them susceptible to Carmilla, giving her easy access to their souls.

Marie-Lydia wasn't easy. To me, she was the daughter I never had—and that I never would have now that I'd moved beyond the natural functions and expectations of a woman. But for one so young and so in need and so deserving of correction, one who could still use her abilities for the greater good of humankind, there was hope.

I would redeem her. She was my passion project. She kept me wondering as I tried to keep from endlessly wandering the depths. Was there a way for me to find my way back to myself, my entire self, freeing myself completely from Carmilla while simultaneously freeing the girl? Something within me—deep within me, beyond the sight or grasp of Carmilla—told me there was a way. And that it involved *Love*.

Janice pulled the car to a complete stop before something that wasn't a red light. Such a change shook me from my reverie.

She'd pulled the car up to a curb on our right and let the vehicle idle. Still staring straight ahead through the windshield, she pointed with her right thumb toward my window.

"Your accommodations for the evening," Janice said, speaking to me for the first time that afternoon.

Looking through the passenger's side window, I narrowed my eyes. A generous path of rectangular pavers led to a tall and wide building, one I immediately took, despite the lack of signage, to be a pricey hotel. A curved, fancy-columned portico lent shade and class to the establishment's front entrance.

"Go to the front desk. Ask for Jaspar."

Another pseudonym, no doubt. Keeping it all in the *J* family. A selection from one of Carmilla's unique brands of magick.

Silently, I slid out of the car. No questions. No parting words. I closed the door gently behind me. Showed no aggression. Only obedience. Compliance.

Toward the hotel's front doors, I picked my way down a broad pathway of crisscrossing pavers—red and black rectangles with deep crevices between. I wanted to curse Carmilla but cursed my high heels instead. Though the establishment's facade spoke of a high-end establishment, the men and women I saw exiting and entering all seemed sensible with their footwear—sneakers and comfortable flats—even if their attire above the ankles was a bit dressier.

The front doors were a series of three: a mostly glass revolving door at the center and, on either side, a set of tinted-glass double doors. A doorperson was stationed next to each set.

To my right, a man; to my left, a woman. Both wore caps and jackets. The man smiled immediately as I passed the portico's columns, entering their space. The woman looked me up and down twice and displayed only a constipated expression when my eyes met hers.

She turned quickly from me, however, when the doors next to her whooshed open, allowing passage to three men in expensive jeans and sports jackets leaving the hotel. The double doors apparently opened automatically when approached from the inside.

I'd been preparing to use the revolving door but, catching sight of the doorman once more, I saw him grasp the gilded handle of the door closest to him and pull it all the way open for me. With a faint smile, I nodded my gratitude as I passed.

Though it wasn't immediately in sight, the front desk wasn't that hard to find. The lobby was busy with folks milling about, chatting, making plans, and people rushing this way and that, making their way to one of the on-site bars, the coffee kiosks, or the concierge's desk. Certainly not overwhelming, but I was surprised at the slight onset of dizziness.

I navigated toward the long mahogany desk and its three black-suited receptionists. One was assisting a pair with check-ins, one was on the phone, and the third was glued to his computer.

I started toward the third, but the second man gestured me over. He hung up his phone as I approached and flashed a professional if joyless smile.

"Uh, hi . . . my . . . I mean . . ." No idea why I was having trouble with my words. Some delayed effect from my earlier therapy session? Or was something in the air, something I couldn't quite detect?

He leaned forward a little, his eyes flicking down and back up. "Are you meeting someone here?"

"Oh, I, uh, yes. How did you—?"

"You're not a guest, and you have no luggage."

Fair enough.

"Name?"

"Uh, Jenny."

"Jenny . . . ?" He dragged the second syllable out for several seconds, expecting me to fill in the blank before he went silent.

"Uhm . . ." I reflexively mimicked the drawn-out sound, unsure how to explain to him that I had no last name. "My name is just—"

His eyes closed as he shook his head. "The name of the party you're meeting."

"Oh." This wasn't going to go much better. "Jaspar."

He smiled again—an expression that found its joy—as he gently nodded, straightening his back and inhaling deeply through his nose. "Ah. I would not have figured . . ." His words trailed off as he picked up the phone, lowered his gaze to the base, and muttered to whomever had picked up on the other side. Gibberish to me.

He hung up the phone and smiled again as he met my eyes. Unmistakable pleasure in his expression. Too much of it for my taste.

He slipped from behind the desk and beckoned me to follow as he wound toward an elevator bank. He made an abrupt turn to the left before we reached it.

Weaving between potted plants and people scurrying this way and that, I didn't lend him my complete attention and thus didn't fully comprehend how we wound up in a dim, narrow pathway that turned right and left and deposited us into a dark-red lit box of an area featuring a single elevator door opposite a framed painting of a sailing ship alone in a stormy sea.

Not exactly a private elevator, I supposed, but certainly an out-of-the-way one. No one was waiting for it. No one had been heading for it or coming from it as he threaded through the narrow hallway. Had the hallway leading here been closed off by a door that I hadn't noticed?

The man pushed the button next to it, and the door slid open immediately. He made a gentlemanly gesture for me to step inside. Once I did, he leaned halfway in, slid a key card into a slot next to the buttons, and pressed the button for the third from the top floor.

Pocketing the key card in his suit's jacket, he said, "She will be waiting for you. Can't miss her."

He winked at me as the door slid shut.

The cab whirred as it carried me upward into who-the-hell-knew-what. During the slow crawl, I noticed the buttons for the top five floors were colored differently from the rest. It took no great leap to guess they were only accessible by key card. I did wonder if the floors were accessible via the other elevators. If so, the receptionist likely didn't want to risk me riding the elevators with others and having them get off on a floor that wasn't meant to accept them. As the elevator door slid open, I saw why that might've been a problem.

Though part of me fought against it, I did step off the elevator, even continued moving forward, into a debauched and raucous throng of men and women in various states of undress and dress-up.

Leather outfits. BDSM attire. Men in studded dog collars. Women in leather bunny masks and elbow gloves. Men in body chains and booty harnesses. Women in lace or fishnet body stockings and thongs and nothing else except the heels on which they strutted their stuff. Many of them wielded all manner of accessories and gadgets, some of which I recognized, a few of which I knew were designed to stimulate pleasure or pleasurable pain.

I'd wandered into a convention of perversion. A ranging party of sexual deviants.

The floor was configured differently from those of the hotels with which I was familiar. No narrow hallway lined with identical, numbered doors on the left and right. The walkway here was wider, and not straight. More of a lazy zigzag, proceeding straight on in one direction for a ways before kinking slightly to the left or right in another direction for a dozen feet, before doing the same in the other direction.

Many of the folks I passed were going about their business, engaged in conversation or making their way—sometimes flamboyantly—from one room to another. A few made eye contact, smiling as they looked me up and down, but I didn't return the assessment, didn't smile, didn't return any greetings.

No one was completely nude or entirely indecent—at least not in the hallways. Inside the rooms, most of which seemed to be suites, it was a different story.

Doors here were broader than I was accustomed to. All were open or nonexistent, making every doorway an invitation. Each was like a portal into another compact world of sensual pleasure, humiliation, overindulgence, degradation, joy, debauchery, and so much more. I barely understood many of the acts I witnessed.

I couldn't help but turn my head this way and that, sometimes to avoid staring too long at a sight I didn't want to see in the first place but also looking for my connect, for whom I had no physical description.

In order to help my connect find me, I figured I needed to make myself more known, getting out of the halls and entering each open door by at least a few paces, in case she happened to be deeper inside one of them. I felt half a dozen steps would be plenty. It was certainly more than enough for me in the first room I tried.

Perched on a long, armless sofa were six women in a line, all in their late twenties or early thirties, each incongruously dressed in a white toga, golden braid belt, and modern chic businesswomen's high heels. They sat in seductive poses, prizes to the eyes of the six slouching, potbellied, or back-hairy middle-aged men who stood in a row before them, licking their lips each time one of the women shifted her legs or touched her hair. Far less modest than the women, the men had dressed down to silk shorts and sandals. Each of the men held a bottle in one hand—differently shaped containers filled with wine, beer, or something else entirely. Their free hands hung at their sides, making no movement—not even a flinch—to touch the woman nearest them.

But this wasn't a staring contest or some version of a peep show.

In short order, the women slowly, seductively removed one of their pumps—each of which was colored some shade of red or purple—and handed it to the wet-lipped man standing directly in front of her. Receiving the so recently worn high-heeled shoe in one hand, each man proceeded to balance it, holding it steady, as he poured his spirits or whatever into the footwear. Then, almost in unison, each of the men lifted the shoe above their eye level, holding it aloft and tilting it as their head bent backward, mouth wide open to receive the liquid momentarily intermingled with a woman's foot funk.

The women watched, seemingly amused, slowly shifting their positions from one seductive pose to another. Finished with their libations, the men proceeded to lick the shoes' soles as if they were licking frosting from a spoon.

Admittedly, I was perversely enthralled—enough so to watch several minutes of the action.

Not so much in the next room, featuring a woman who had apparently stomped around in a knee-deep pit of peanut butter and melted chocolate—or danced in it, judging by the splotches on her legs and thighs. However the sweet paste had made its way onto her body, she was now relaxing on a cocktail ottoman, shifting her position ever so slightly as four individuals—two women and two men—licked the gunk off her feet and calves.

In another room, a woman sat on a throne, smoking and putting out the cigarettes on the skin of the men and women she had chained to the chair, lying at her feet, tight and spiked leather collars around their necks. Mere seconds of watching this prompted an image of Carmilla to flash in my mind.

I quickly turned to leave, only to wander into a suite where a group of naked men were being wrapped in cellophane and another group, previously wrapped, were being stripped of their skin-tight coverings by nude women wild with blades wedged between their fingers.

All these fetishes on display. All these *weirds* indulging in such. Had Carmilla placed me here so I might visually receive some sort of message or just to display some of the types she harbored for future use in whatever other schemes she had going?

Either way, on the surface, it was supposed to mess with me. Provoke a state of mind. Shock. Anger at her. Disgust. Revulsion at the people around me. Embarrassment. Shame, reflecting back on me.

I wasn't white bread. Or vanilla. She had to know that. Just as she had to know that as much as I'd put up with her attitude and antics over the last several weeks, thrusting me into a kinky environment was unlikely to achieve whatever results she wanted.

Though I began to second guess myself, ponder more on her possible motives, the more I saw.

Full body lathering and shaving.

Clamps everywhere. Chains and whips.

Lashings. Pinchings. Slappenings.

Impossible piercings. Genital torture.

All the while, many men and some women looked at me. Not like an object to be fondled and played with. More like something to be devoured, consumed. Softening their eyes. Licking their lips. Smiling and revealing clenched teeth.

I was seeing far too much. Even some of the glimpses were overwhelming.

Yet, while turning to exit a room disgusting beyond words, my gaze fell on a woman from whom I couldn't look away.

She was garbed in pink combat boots with black soles and laces, sheer black nylon stockings with lace tops, dare-you pink leather panties, and—covering most of her torso, from above her navel to the base of her neck—some kind of vest, a mesmerizing iridescent pink in tone. Black leather pads with silver spikes were fastened to her knees and elbows. And framing a makeup-free, naturally beautiful brown face was a stunningly elaborate headdress that put me in the mind of Cleopatra.

The room's doorway framed her entire body, blocking my exit. She showed no intent of moving as her beguiling eyes locked with mine momentarily.

She looked me up and down as I had her, fleered, then purred, "Hello, dear," with more than a hint of mockery.

My teeth clenched before I swallowed back my initial response. "And you are?"

"Call me Jaspar."

Reflexively, I again assessed the package before me. After all I'd seen today, she still wasn't what I was expecting.

"Follow me." She turned a shoulder and wove through the others in the hall, not bothering to keep a delicate pace.

No request for my name. No extension of a hand to shake. No warmth or politeness at all. *That* I was kind of expecting.

She led me to a closed door that, opened, revealed a staircase. To be used in case of fire, I suspected. And I guessed the revelers took fire safety seriously as there were none hanging out or playing on the stairs.

With no words, Jaspar took me up one flight and onto a floor hosting more deviants. But from what I glimpsed, from what I could even feel in the air, these seemed of a different sort. This was a playground for those more into art than rank debauchery.

Jaspar led me into a dim and perfumed suite where I had no choice but to practically wade through—slowly, trancelike—a group of muscular men, clothed only in their neatly trimmed beards, who drew thick, jam-like calligraphy on each other, painting each other with esoteric messages that, once finished, others—their audience, their admirers, their supplicants, men and women armed with knives, spoons, and forks—interpreted and erased, scraping off the thick, sweet lines and licking their utensils clean before proceeding to pair off and engage in the acts the coded messages had instructed.

I'll admit it was all hypnotic. And all of it occurred in what seemed an impossibly large room. I must've taken my time to marvel, for I reached the other end of the room and found that I'd lost sight of Jaspar.

"Jenny."

I turned left at the sound of my given name and saw a door that I hadn't noticed before. Jaspar was clutching the handle with her left hand and waving me over with her right. I made my way over and followed her in.

A bedroom. Empty. And seemingly clean. Jaspar halted after entering the room just enough for me to step in. I stepped farther in, looking around as she closed the door, locked it, and stood in front of it, hands on her hips, assessing me anew, as if there was better light in this room to do so.

I ignored her as I continued looking around. The bedroom had its own bathroom.

"Your quarters for the evening," Jaspar said.

I'd assumed as much, which was why it was so important I ensured the place would be clean enough for me to shut my eyes with little worry. Adjusting my vision, I ran it through every necessary range as I scanned the bathroom, searching for any trace of filth, any hidden cameras, anything else that didn't lend itself to my safety.

"And you've come to us without any change of clothes. Or toiletries."

It wasn't put forward as a question—just a statement of fact.

"Knowing Carmilla, she probably scripted an entire beauty regimen for you, one to accentuate whatever abilities you have, and whatever else she's seen within you."

Involuntarily, I nodded as I exited the bathroom. I then continued my scan of the bedroom.

Jaspar continued her unpleasantness. "You're to use a specific body wash and shampoo, lotions and makeup you can't get at your local pharmacy. What's more, I'm sure there's a ritual at play. Each time, you must use a specific amount of these products, apply them in a set order. All of it is an unconscious routine by this point."

I stopped looking around, narrowed my gaze on her. "And what is your point, if I may ask?"

"We have none of whatever she had you using. And you brought none with you. Though you are for all intents and purposes *hers*, you are not as enslaved to her as her others."

"I would prefer not being referred to as a slave."

"And I would prefer that you not be here at all, but . . ." She tilted her head to the left and lazily twirled her right hand in the air.

"For one of her acolytes," I said, "you seem pretty flip about her and how she operates."

"I'm not one of her acolytes. Just one of her business associates. She is paying us to keep you for the evening."

I didn't care to ask how much.

"And, with respect to how *we* operate, just know that you'll be okay here, so long as you don't leave the room for the rest of the evening. Lock the door behind me immediately, and no one will even know you're here."

Without another word or even a dismissive snort, she unlocked the door, opened it, and closed it behind her, all seemingly in one graceful motion. Maybe she'd been a dancer in her previous life. Hell, maybe she still was.

After wasting one moment on that thought, I rushed forward and followed her advice, remembering how I hadn't even seen the door from the outside until she called my attention to it, while touching the handle.

Jaspar may not have been in Carmilla's camp, but she undoubtedly had some neat tricks of her own.

Regardless, my trust was hard to come by. I resolved to spend more time checking and rechecking the room for any potential tricks that might be detrimental to my well-being. In my position, one could never be too careful.

I WOKE up to a gray day, serenaded by a murder of crows.

Serenaded by a murder.

A chorus of killers? Beyond-sea sirens? A living-dead choral group singing an invitation?

I was underhearing and overthinking. Let the eyes have their turn . . .

The sky was overcast. The field around me, an ashy green.

The cawing black birds perched among the dull green leaves of red maples.

The oppressed greenness and overwhelming grayness struck me more than the fact that I had awakened in a far different environment from that in which I was last conscious.

This was no surprise. The witch liked to play these sorts of tricks. It was supposed to instill the fact that she could move me around like a chess piece, at any time she liked.

She'd never openly admit that, of course. Displacement and the derangement of senses—her acolytes and other would-be servants needed to get used to them if they were to survive in this world. And in the world the witch sought to create.

Though my muscles were a little tight and my joints a little stiff (nothing a quick round of stretching couldn't fix), I figured orientation wouldn't be a problem for me. There was, however, an immediate challenge: an unfamiliar name lingering in the moss-green space between my conscious and subconscious.

Campbell.

A reverend, I somehow knew. Presumably a reverend affiliated with the church I saw off in the distance to my right. The only structure in view.

Carmilla had said something about making a confession. As I stretched my limbs, holding my gaze on the structure as much as possible, I knew this wasn't a Catholic church. In what other sort did one make confession?

I supposed in whatever sort of church or other structure the confessor wanted, so long as the confession was only thought and wrestled with internally.

I began toward the building, wondering what day it was. Couldn't be Sunday. I saw no cars. I figured this early, there'd at least be a few belonging to people getting the place ready for services. Likely wasn't Saturday, either, for a similar reason. Even if this particular church didn't offer Saturday services, there would still likely be someone on the premises to tidy up or tend to other matters before the biggest day of the week.

I'd no watch. No phone. Nothing on me but a black hourglass over-bust corset, black leather. Shoulders, arms, and legs were bare. Around the waist, the leather gave way to a short, lacy skirt, under which I wore nothing but a thong—black, of course. I was shocked to find my feet sheathed in black ballet slippers rather than stiletto peep-toes.

Someone cleverer than me might have been able to tell the day of the week by the air's temperature, the direction of the wind, the moss on the trees and the way their leaves danced—taking all that and intuitively running it through some formula to get a correct answer. Me, I needed a calendar.

Or just a passerby willing to answer the question. But even as I got within a couple dozen paces of the church, it seemed not just empty but as if it had been deserted for some time.

It was a good-size structure, maybe able to seat about five hundred worshippers comfortably.

Carefully, I circled the building through wild weeds and unmanicured grass, trying to peer through the stained-glass and regular windows (equally hopeless) while minding my surroundings.

I was surprised none of the windows were shattered. Less surprised to find myself almost stumbling over some of the debris hidden in the grass. Broken bricks, sticks, and plastic bottles, some half-filled with murky liquids. People had been around. People without a care for the property. Had all of them been respectful enough to leave the building alone? Or had some of them taken shots only to find the place was built better than they assumed?

Was there any chance of anyone coming back today to try again?

As I cased the place, I watched for approaching bodies

(human, beast, and other) and listened for footsteps not my own as well as any sounds of life beyond the chirping birds.

Nothing.

As far as I knew, I was alone.

I circled back to the church's front and approached the double doors of the main entrance, lifting my hand toward the handle only to hesitate halfway. After taking a moment to think about it, I circled back around the building, heading for a door on the church's right side.

I wasn't necessarily looking for the element of surprise. But even though my intuition couldn't tell me the day of the week, it was pretty good about telling me when to be cautious.

Before I reached the door, I glanced to either side and behind me before bending the light around my body, making myself invisible to normal human sight.

The door was unlocked, making me further suspicious.

Make confession . . . What the hell did that mean, exactly?

Maintaining my invisibility, I gently closed the door behind me and found myself in a kitchen area. Dim. Humid. Dusty. No sign any food had been in here for some time. None fit for humans, that is.

The competing scents were rot and decaying flesh, interlaced with traces of feces. Animals had gotten in before me. Done their business and gotten back out. Or gone farther in, to explore and die.

I crept over uncarpeted, creaking floorboards as I left the kitchen and entered a short corridor of open and closed doors. I peered into the shadows of the nearest open one and adjusted my vision so I could see as well if not better than any nocturnal hunter. Finding nothing more interesting than broken furniture and cobwebs, I turned my attention to the nearest closed door, adjusting my vision again as I stepped closer.

It was easy enough to see through the solid wood and just

as easy to determine that there were no bodies, living or dead, inside the room.

I continued the routine—keeping the closed doors closed, inching a foot or two into the rooms with open doors, and more than once having to pinch my nose to prevent a sneeze from responding to the abundant dust—until I left the corridor with the same feeling I'd had when entering the building. No humans were here, but there was some danger.

The corridor deposited me into another, wider passageway. To my left, at the far end, were the double doors of the front entrance. To my right, the sanctuary.

Maintaining my invisibility, I proceeded to my right.

A faint but distinct buzzing became more apparent with each step. Not like flies or bees, but similar enough to put me in mind of insects. As my eyes were focused on my destination (also darting this way and that for any potential surprises), my ears zeroed in on the sound.

It wasn't a consistent, even-toned drone. It did not rise much in volume as I neared the sanctuary's threshold, but there were noticeable peaks and valleys. Breaks, even. I had the impression that I was listening to the collected conversations of a crowd, muted by its distance from me.

The thought was pushed further back in my mind when I fully entered the sanctuary and laid eyes on its main feature.

On a raised platform, behind a lectern, stood a tall figure, its long, thin hands grasping either side of the reading platform.

I hesitated to call the "it" a man, though it had seemed to be —once. Draped in a predominantly black vestment ornamented with gold, thin-lined calligraphy, the figure's head was more corpselike than not. Skin was present (tight, wrinkled, and gray) as was hair (a thinning mass of white strands that moved with a breeze I didn't feel), but he seemed frozen in place. Beyond those errant strands, no part of him shifted by any fraction. Not that I could see.

Did he see me? He had eyes—brown irises, yellowish whites—looking directly at me. But as I neared, the eyes stayed the same. Didn't narrow or widen or even blink.

I rolled the dice and unbent the light surrounding me, dropping my shroud of invisibility. It changed nothing. Not with his eyes at least.

As I crept forward—down the incline, toward the lectern, trying to determine if he was even breathing—I inadvertently noticed strands thinner than his hair, far more translucent, and much longer. Numerous thin lines—wires, maybe—that enwrapped him and trailed off, straight and narrow, to attach to the ceiling, the lectern, parts of the floor and the walls nearest him.

Inching closer, I saw more and more of them stretching every which way. I adjusted my sight—telescoped, microscoped —and focused on the flecks I detected moving up and down the lines and crawling across the tall figure's body.

Spiders. Or approximations of such. They were the source of the buzzing, the only sounds not made by me in this sanctuary.

I stopped about a dozen paces away from the lectern, took a breath, then pushed up off the floor, levitating, pausing to hover at eye level with the corpse draped in faintly glowing webs and crawling with living, glittery specks.

I thought the communication would be limited to them, until a guttural sound filled the sanctuary.

Reflexively, my head whipped about, searching for the source, for the potential danger. My muscles tensed, my hands at the ready to punch, claw, or manipulate light in my favor. Blinding, burning—doing whatever I could do and needed to do to stun or stop an oncoming threat.

But aside from my own and the spiderlike specks, there was no movement in this space. My focus settled back on face of the man behind the lectern.

His lips hadn't moved. None of him had moved. But I wondered if he had been the ultimate source of the harsh noise. He or something using him.

I refocused eyes and ears on the busy motes, the creatures crawling all over him and the wires which, though translucent, had a faint orange-brownish tint.

"*Confess . . .*"

A chorus of whispered voices, few of them sounding totally human but enough of them for me to hear the command clearly, plenty of them to lend the demand some authority.

So many whispered in unison that I was stunned. My mouth opened reflexively in response, but I uttered no sound. I simply hovered in space, gaping, my eyes widened by the word, my first greeting of the day. A sinister version of good morning.

My lack of satisfactory reaction seemed to stir the stale air. I felt gusts of hot and cold breezes crisscrossing my body as I picked up earthy aromas, their prominence rapidly increasing.

The combination had the (likely intended) effect of making me feel as if my burial were imminent, and a fiery Heaven or ice-cold Hell (or both in rapid order) would soon greet me.

"*Confess,*" the chorus repeated, louder, more insistent.

"I—" I stopped myself to swallow. "What would you like to hear?"

"Who do you think you are? Why do you think you've come?"

I hesitated, parted my lips to respond, then hesitated again. Questions and answers whirled in my head. Many of the questions similar but slightly different, not unlike the individual voices making up the chorus. I had to be careful with my answer, but also correct. Honest. I knew if I answered falsely, I'd not only be found out but might wind up buried after all.

"I am a divine being but a broken one. I've fallen into indentured servitude to the witch Carmilla Jones. I wish to avoid becoming her unwitting slave. I think I've come here as a first step on my path to complete freedom from her."

For a moment, there was silence. Even the spiderlike specks' faint buzzing ceased.

Then, in front of me, the corpse reverend's eyes glowed. His tree-bark irises cranked to beet red.

"Then, now"—a harsh voice boomed, enveloping me—"by the power vested"—sandpapering my skin and gnawing at my senses—"and divested"—as if some grand unseen presence were consuming me—"I pronounce you—"

A shower of white light dazzled me a moment before I found myself engulfed in a dull, intangible amber, a radiance that rapidly snuffed out my energy as my consciousness dimmed.

WHEN I CAME TO, I was blind. And deaf.

But I had enough sense—intuition, really—to know I was in a cage. Some kind of enclosure. And uncomfortably warm.

My eyes were open but, rather than darkness, I saw nothing but an unbroken whiteness. I didn't even see my own body. But I knew I was floating. Undulating.

I waited for a sound. A loud tone. A low hum. A distant ringing. But there was nothing.

Not until four gray smudges appeared before me in a row, evenly spaced.

The smudges elongated, widened slightly, taking on more definition and color, and soon resolved themselves into four figures floating in white space, like me, but seeming much more at home in it.

All humanoid, nude, and strangely androgynous. No prominent genitalia, but based on their body frames, three tended male and one female. Respectively, the three males were pale blue, medium red, and purplish gray; the female, forest green. None displayed any body hair except on their heads—close-cropped hair of hues matching their skin tones.

Though their bodies' features were ill defined, their faces were anything but. As they drifted closer to me, three glared and one—the purplish-gray one—seemed amused.

Beyond them, from all sides, I heard sounds—moaning and groaning, multiple voices—all of it removed, as if coming from inside a baseball stadium while we five hovered at the far edge of its parking lot.

At a certain distance, the four stopped—hovering momentarily, their faces unchanging—until the purplish-gray one floated forward, closer to me, as the other three receded slightly, arranging themselves so that the medium-red one was to his right, the forest-green one was to his left, and the pale-blue one was slightly above.

I had a good view of all their bodies but not a single visual hint of my own. A different kind of manacles, I supposed. Rather than chain me up, my body was rendered invisible to my eyes. I'd just enough sensation to believe I had a body, but I wasn't sure. I was only certain that, if I did, I lacked the ability to move it in any way.

As the smirking leader and his three firm-lipped or scowling attendants fixed their gazes on me, the whiteness behind them evaporated like mist, giving solid view to a congregation of naked bodies—human bodies of every human color, grinding, packed closely together along with longer, twisting, tubular objects of various shades of blue, brown, and gray.

I couldn't turn around or do much to look up or down, but the writhing bodies seemed a massive wall without end, possibly curving to my left and right, above and below, placing the five of us within a grotesque sphere made up of hundreds if not thousands of bodies—entangled, writhing, moaning—flesh sweating, slapping and rubbing against one another and, many of them, against what I soon recognized as slime-slicked tentacles, giant-squid size.

Amid this hellish orgy, the four before me glowed with a pale aura, making them easier to distinguish and, mercifully, making it easier for me to lend them my attention.

Or maybe I was too quick to think of mercy.

The four bodies took on new attributes. Clothing, in a sense—though not in what anyone sane would regard as sensible.

The reddish one's once-smooth skin was now knotted with bluish spiders. The forest-green one was crawling with red and black ants. The pale-blue one's body was busy with dark-green bees.

And their purplish-gray leader had become a beacon for tiny, dragonfly-winged scorpions—dozens and dozens of them— which seemed to emerge from unseen portals just a few feet away from his presence. They flew to him, landed, crawled about, and occasionally rose a few inches off the skin's surface, paddling their wings furiously, before landing again, giving their wings a rest as they scuttled about.

Maybe the mercy I'd briefly pondered had actually been lent to the orgiastic bodies. They weren't within reaching distance of the four. No arachnids or insects for them. Only cephalopods for their enjoyment.

The purplish-gray one neared me by another foot or so, grinning.

"Hello, Ms. Applebaum."

A booming voice, one that the orgiastic moans and other exclamations of joyous pain didn't come close to drowning out.

"Or maybe Applebaum belongs to another life, and you've grown quite comfortable with *Jenny?*"

I'd have to take it on faith that Applebaum had been my original name. Or that of my husband. One of my one-time therapists . . .

"Jenny No-Name. Jenny No-Way. Jenny No-Real-Plan-or-Good-Destination."

"I—" I stuttered as if my teeth were chattering. "I confessed. Told you—"

"What you thought we wanted to hear. But, while you can, you should hear and understand this: we know why you're here. And we know you better than you do."

I had no argument. And the man looked like he was eager to keep on, so I reacted with no words, no sounds, allowing him to continue on his desired verbal path.

"You're like the piece in some game between us. Us and the witch Carmilla. Switching from our possession to hers and back again. You must like being played."

I didn't, and I had a sense I was being toyed with now.

"You have me at a disadvantage at the moment," I said, "but I was never before in your possession. I don't know who you are."

"Of course, you do. With little effort, I can read enough of your mind to know you haven't forgotten meeting our great Doctor Jim Linkins several years ago, when you were killing time in a bar. It's still quite vivid to you. And I'm sure you remember what happened after he determined that you had consumed large amounts of red ice."

I hesitated. "No. I don't." The term wasn't completely foreign, but damned if I knew what it meant.

"The memories are there, Ms. Apple—I mean, *Jenny.*"

"I don't have them."

The man inched closer as his eyes glowed cherry red. His seemed to be peering directly into mine—or whatever I was using to see. If I had eyes, they had no lids. I couldn't blink or shut him out.

In the moments of silence, the moans and cries of ecstasy around us cranked up. Their volume lowered again when the man smiled. "The witch really did a number on you, didn't she?"

I wouldn't argue.

"Yes, she really did . . . Very well. Let's say I take you at your word. You want your final freedom from Carmilla."

"I do."

"And there's nothing I can see within you that contradicts that desire, nothing but the intangible chains the witch has woven through your being, the shackles that are partially fastened on your soul. What do you say we undo them altogether, by stirring up some memories she'd prefer remain buried and settled?"

I didn't necessarily trust Carmilla, but it wasn't clear to me what this one was up to. Whatever memories had been laid to rest, maybe some of them had been buried for a reason. Buried by me. Hiding them from Carmilla to keep her from manipulating, gaining greater portions of my soul.

But I didn't see what I could do to resist here either. For the moment, I'd have to fight to remain calm and centered in the face of anything rotten and resist the urge to believe any foul lies about me he might try to convince me were hidden truths.

"You are familiar with the White Fire Virus," he said. "What some of its possessors can do. The ones who survive the infection, that is. The survivors—those who are able to retake control of their minds and bodies from the parasites infesting them, and those who are able to maintain supremacy over such

—they possess some superb abilities. I believe we've yet to see the limits.

"There are others—some of them my associates, some of them clients—who desire similar abilities for themselves without taking on the nasty business of the virus. Abilities that will meet the possible limits of the virus and exceed them. And that's where the laced elixirs came in."

I heard myself saying "The Trinfecta . . ." Memories were being stirred, slowly but surely.

The man nodded. "Our organization. Years ago, we developed crystals that could be liquified and ingested and, while being digested, would permeate the imbiber's body, eventually reconstituting. Billions of minuscule crystals embedded throughout the body, able to understand and react to their possessor's thoughts and will. Not quite sentient, but able to tap into their possessor's deepest desires and wishes and act accordingly, independent of conscious thought."

"And this," I said, "this is what was perfected in me."

The man released a booming laugh, as did the three behind him, though theirs were somewhat muted yet more derisive in tone.

"You are far from perfect. A long way from unique. But you were one of the first. An unwitting participant in the early phases.

"You see, what I described to you was what the program eventually became. You imbibed before the White Fire Virus was widely known or understood. The virus itself was in its infancy.

"In those days, the head of the project was an introspective fellow, a reclusive sort, and truly hands on, insisting on doing as much of the work himself—by himself—as possible. He was the kind to make breakthroughs and discoveries and not tell anyone.

"The rogue was actually working off site, outside the premises of our laboratories, when he half created, half discovered the element, something that we would eventually term 'red ice.' It was too unstable for him to use on himself, so he set out to procure some test subjects. He wouldn't settle for just anyone; he had specific types in mind.

"Others at the Trinfecta found out what he was doing. He somehow found out we were coming for him, and when. So he spirited his samples away from his lab to a friend of his, the owner of the bar.

"Somehow, this formula, some of it, ended up in your drink. The drinks of others, too, but it seems you ingested the most. Minuscule crystals. In liquid, they'd appear very little different from the bubbles in a glass of champagne—though, looking closely, you'd notice a slight red tinge. They're not colorless."

"'Somehow,'" I said, "seems more like 'intentionally.' Why would he, why would anyone stash this stuff at a bar, of all places? And how would it end up in our drinks if vodka, beer, and whatever the hell else we were drinking had been bottled and sealed off premises?"

"Likely the crystals were stored in the ice kept in the well, deep under it, and whatever they were packaged in busted, mixing the crystals with the ice."

"I call that BS." He had to be making this up, trying to trick me, swerve me from believing I was what I really was.

"Call it what you want. Doesn't change the end result."

I said nothing to that. What happened in the bar—he made it seem like too much of an accident. I felt much differently but couldn't exactly tell why. Instead, I wondered about the abilities. *Exceeding the limits* . . . I knew much of what I could do. Now I couldn't help but wonder if resurrecting oneself from the dead was another ability. It would go a long way toward explaining our awakening in the field all those years ago.

But I realized I was letting my guard down. Letting myself believe this one's words. His lies.

"The White Fire parasites evolved in the bodies of their carriers. The crystals did too. And you—you are one of the few survivors, one of the few from those very early days of experimentation and unwilling participants."

"And you're still experimenting," I said. "On me. On others. That's what you're about to say, right? You want me to participate in some grand scheme."

"Actually, yes. We need you to help us locate our beloved mentor. Nothing more, nothing less."

I felt like calling BS again but remained silent.

"The doctor the witch is trying to find, and who we are also trying to find, disappeared while deep into conducting some monumental experiments. These three behind me are imperfect versions. Part of one of the doctor's greatest unfinished experiments."

"Versions of what?"

"Versions of a purified humanity. Virgins, of a sort."

"Right—and what the hell should I care about them?" I heard myself saying before I could waste a thought on it.

"Why, that's rude. They certainly care about you. They've done everything they can to help you see your way to a heavenly existence. Don't you recognize them?"

I couldn't resist the invitation to look at the three more closely. Gradually, I did recognize them—their vague faces—as guests at the wedding. *My* wedding. They'd also been the three to laugh, to boisterously enjoy the hilarity of my new husband insulting me over cake. My husband . . . whose face I couldn't remember.

The man in the bar, whose face . . .

Could they . . . ?

My husband and the bar burner—one and the same.

No. That couldn't be. But these three . . . Their behavior had been infectious among the guests. Spreading like a virus, until all the others were essentially clones of the three.

A rudimentary smile spread across the purplish-gray one's face. I'd sudden flashes, intermittent impressions of him wearing the same garb as my wedding's officiant.

"Our brilliant Doctor Linkins had the will and was refining the ways he might create perfect versions of humanity. He wanted to begin small, taking a few natural performers and reformers—activist artists with hearts of gold—investing them with abilities that, when put to proper use, would making them guiding lights, perfect versions of the ideal human. Saviors don't fall out of the sky. And if humankind can't come together to save themselves, then those of us with the will and the way are obligated to create and nurture those who will bring salvation to us all.

"We need our glorious doctor to help us finish what he started. He is calling to us through you. And we are doing our best to respond."

His words, all benevolence and spring sunshine to a lazy listener. I wasn't sure why—in the middle of a hellish orgy, being stared down by colorful wretches—he expected me to believe his motives were purely altruistic. But I wasn't even about to pretend there was a fraction of goodness in them.

"You're full of it."

"And you were once replete with a soul, which Carmilla wants—fully." He chuckled, then cocked his head. "You confessed you're aware she's out to steal your entire soul. You think it's been your valiant efforts, your talents, that have kept her from succeeding. Right? The piece of your essence that she has, entrapped in one of her many gemstones, it keeps you from touching her, hurting her. When you look at the others in her orbit, those who are hers completely, how do you—*broken,* as you admitted—how do you think you've been so clever as to keep her at bay? That's us. Our influence. Without our continued protection, there's nothing stopping her from possessing your entire soul. She'll steal it all."

I hesitated again. I wanted to argue but couldn't. Instead, I said, "And you. What are you out to steal?"

"We simply want your assistance—your willing assistance— to continue on with saving humankind. With us, you continue as you began, on the path to something greater. For yourself and for others."

The path to something greater. Just like the path I'd thought I'd been on, until that wedding. A wedding I was no longer even sure had been a reality. Had it just been a ceremony, part of my participation in their experiments?

"Come now," he said, "you have always felt the urge to continue on with us. You have always considered yourself a higher being, knew you were great and destined to be greater. After you first ingested the red ice, it seemed like some blessed angel residing deep within you gazed at your soul, fell in love, intermingled, copulated, then sneezed, speckling your skin with the results. This is what you've believed. Deep down. That was the aftermath of your alleged *death*. Right?"

Yes. That is how I'd felt—when I had a body. When I'd come to terms with my new, reborn self. But now, seemingly absent a body . . .

The moaning and groaning around me seemed to increase. The slick bodies became more agitated, as if simultaneously discovering and breaking new boundaries of their lust. Yet the three hovering behind the purplish-gray one—the doctor's "virgins, of a sort"—they couldn't have been more silent.

If the wedding ceremony had just been part of the experiment, a ceremony attended by a whole legion of such as these three, what did that make me to them? What was I really to them? A facilitator. Some kind of sexual tool. Erotic equipment. An object of no real respect from them whatsoever.

"Now," their leader said, "with your affirmation, your honest assent to cooperate, we'll release you, leave this nether realm together, and continue where we left off."

Where we'd left off. Absence. Absent of body and mind—when I'd been dead. Allegedly dead or not, I'd still had a soul. As I mostly did now.

Pushing my attention past the hovering four, I focused on the writhing, moaning wall of bodies, took full consideration of my situation.

I was here for a reason. Carmilla's reason. The witch knew I would end up in this exact predicament or an approximate one. Being here, to observe and absorb, would somehow aid our mutual goal of awakening the girl.

As I concentrated more and more on the walls of bodies and tentacles—ignoring whatever the purplish-gray one had begun shouting—I gradually understood. Having me spend the night at the hotel's pop-up sex festival hadn't been to torture me. It had been to mess with my mind, yes. But for the sake of preparation.

The witch-girl knew I would end up here. Knew I could get out of it.

The four perhaps thought by depriving me of a body, they made me was powerless. They likely thought the crystals—the most visible signs of what they termed "red ice"—were my greatest asset. When in my body, the crystals certainly assisted my manipulation of light, but I'd spent enough time out of my body to know quite a bit about what I was truly capable of.

Presently, we were in a dimension slightly removed, by a metaphorical curtain or two, from familiar Reality. Carmilla, possessing a piece of my soul, had been able to jerk me out of the hotel, placing me in the vicinity of the church. Possessing a much greater share of the essence of my own consciousness, I knew I could kiss goodbye to all this.

The purplish-gray one had unknowingly provided a hint by mocking what I've believed, deep down . . . *Memories.* Significant components of my soul.

He had tried to stir them. I couldn't move—had no eyes or ears to shut—but I could delve into myself, deep into and through my memories. Blanking out everything beyond as I went deeper.

Deeper.

Back to an old therapy session.

A discussion of family. Bloodlines.

"My family . . . I mean, what is there to say? They died when I was young. Eleven. Then I was raised by an uncle. A man who supported me well through college."

"And after?"

"I cut him off. After I got my first job, you see. I was determined to make it on my own. With whatever I earned. Through my own effort and labor."

That story may or may not have been true. That therapist—real, or Trinfecta scientist? I went further on, even deeper, landing on another foundational memory.

My husband. He dropped dead one day. Food poisoning, apparently. Odd, considering he was eating a meal—we were eating a meal—that he prepared. Chicken and rice dinner. Nothing fancy. Neither pufferfish nor gas station sushi. He'd gone through the usual cycles of vomiting and diarrhea, practically camping out in the bathroom that evening. He'd thought the internal purification rituals would run their course in about twenty-four hours. But I woke up the next morning and almost tripped over his cold, stiff body.

Another memory. A poisonous one. A lie. A falsehood. I pushed past it, excavated deeper, with a greater ferocity.

Powered by more than a slight sense of desperation, I uncovered memories at an increasing speed, traveling through the familiar and unfamiliar pasts of my person, going beyond them, until I reached the point beyond images and words. Pure music. Music that, as my travels changed course, inspired spontaneous lyrics that paradoxically were sung to me as they came from me.

> No matter how much water,
> my head still spins—
> wine and water, water and wine.
> All those crushed grapes, their wills
> spilled to me, spun out and back in
> to mind, until it was spent,
> exhausted, allowed a drain down my spine
> igniting, brighting, spiting me,
> my wanted self, spitting in Love's closed eyes
> ending up in my soul; down in spirit.
> Firewater floods senses, muds the extras,
> Promising only rinses—

As the nearly incomprehensible song faded, I felt something lashing at me—at the body I still wasn't sure I had—until I felt, distinctly, firmly: tentacles grasping, wrapping around my form, squeezing and pulling me in some direction, *multiple* directions, this way and that, before flinging me, plunging me into a mass of agitated bodies, a copulating frenzy of madwomen and madmen who made me a part of their mad play while ripping me apart until blackness overtook me.

But I wasn't absent consciousness.

I was aware I was in a black void. I had no sensation of a body, but I had thoughts. Thoughts that considered my position and then considered how I might find my way out.

Through psychological therapy, I had learned about the brain, how it works, how it works with our senses to help us get an understanding of our surroundings. I learned about how important consciousness is for modeling the environment and the self. I came to understand how I could use consciousness on *my* self to move from one environment to another.

Memories are oriented toward the past.

Perceptions are oriented toward the present.

Expectations are oriented toward the future.

It was to my psychological and physical benefit that I understand these processes. Integrating past sensory experiences (memories, honest to the best of their abilities), controlling, using them wisely, one could create simulations about what is out there beyond the self and what to reasonably anticipate in the near future. For most, these simulations essentially remain hallucinations, relatively controlled and constantly updating based on sensory signals, limited to the mind. One of my talents could go much further, manipulating light, time, and space—all to only a limited extent, but often just enough.

The more I considered what I'd truly learned from my past therapies—well beyond the details of the sessions themselves—the more my thoughts seemed to sharpen, poking at the blackness, letting light peek through. More and more and more, I shredded the blackness and found myself—me, my body, naked —kneeling on a plain.

It was similar to the plain on which I and my barmates had awoken all those years ago. But now, I was alone. Now, I was in the crystal-flecked body I had so recently left, which was much different in appearance than it had been last time I was here. But "here" wasn't that place.

During the process of my escape, my soul had found its way back into my body and situated both in an environment I modeled based on that which had been the starting point for my new life. "Here" was a realm removed from familiar Reality, separated from it by two or a few multidimensional veils.

What were my expectations? Freedom from the four. Freedom from Carmilla. Maybe she was near. Through the separating veils. Maybe this was the starting point for me to ambush her, take back the piece of my soul that I now realized —thanks to my most recent tormentor—was encased within one of her jewels. Perhaps one of her sparkly rings.

I just had to find the right veils and pierce them to get to her.

I glanced about. In Reality, this place had been in the vicinity of vineyards. Favorite hangouts of the witch. She owned a stake in some wineries. Maybe not the one I'd been to before, but what about the one the others had found their way to all those years ago?

I pushed up to my feet, still looking around, enjoying the breezes playing on my bare skin as I tried to get oriented. In which way had that other group traveled all those years ago?

Believing I'd found it, I began walking.

After a dozen steps, I noticed others enjoying the air's currents. Insects. And long glistening strands. Squiggly contrails that slid in and out of visibility, depending on how the light hit them. I batted away the few bugs that crossed my path; the strands were tougher, sticking to my skin and resisting repeated attempts to wipe them off.

But I kept going, proceeding a few dozen more steps, as the population of insects increased, stirring me to take greater notice. I stopped altogether when I realized they weren't behaving like any insects with which I was familiar.

I adjusted my vision, looked closer.

Worms.

A quarter inch long. Hundreds of them. Airborne. All around me. Hovering, writhing, twisting and squirming in space, singly or in pairs, sometimes three or four stuck together, writhing and rubbing against one another. All of them spun out fine lines of glistening, golden silk, several inches of it before snipping, letting the silk loose to float on the breeze as the wriggling worms themselves zigzag-darted off to do the same in another spot nearby.

I didn't stop moving, but I wondered about these others.

This place was a part of my consciousness, in part woven by it and remaining somewhat connected to it. But it was also its own place, almost like a shelter or house I'd built using pieces of my own body, its upkeep and maintenance determined by the state of my own health. Where had the insects and strands come from? What were their purpose? Had some part of me that remained hidden willed them into existence?

Ruminating on them led me down a branching path. Could I exist, even for a short moment, in two different states at two different times, yet somehow remain fully connected, simultaneously aware of and active in both conditions, both places?

I reached nowhere close to a conclusion before a low, distant whistling sound prodded me to lift my chin and look up to the sky, whose color was tinting increasingly toward aqua.

Three glowing dots hovered high in the firmament but—once my eyes found them—descended rapidly, increasing in size and taking on shape and colors as they fell, seemingly straight down and at a good distance from me.

The moment I conjured the impression they were sparks dropped from the sky, accumulating and tumbling into glistening marbles—miniature suns mating with equally small moons—they paused in midair and changed trajectory, still descending, still growing, yet now approaching, as if rolling down a ramp that led directly to me.

The sky also took a turn, acquiring long vaporous streaks

tinted in hues of orange and red against a heavenly backdrop that seemed more suited for a body of water.

The large spheres ceased their fast-paced descent when they were just a few yards away from me. They hovered about a quarter mile from the ground. I'd only a moment to marvel at the texture of the spheres before they burst, revealing the figures they held inside.

I telescoped my vision and examined the three. The *same* three. The imperfect versions.

They appeared as I'd last seen them. On the right, the pale-blue one's body was still thick with green bees. Bluish spiders crawled about the medium-reddish one in the middle. The feminine forest-green one on the left harbored masses of red and black ants.

But as they hovered, their bodies took on more definition, revealing well-developed musculature and making no secret of their genders; their faces became even more distinct, betraying an age range from upper thirties to lower forties; and long strips of ragged cloth unspooled from their backs—below the neck, above the waist.

Several long, wavering strips flowed from each of them, trailing and fluttering in a strong wind I did not feel. At a finger's snap, the banners seemed to catch fire, burning without being consumed.

Fading to a new hue every few seconds, the flames asserted a multitude of colors, conveyed an array of emotions, and instilled within me a range of helpful, hopeful, hateful, hurtful feelings—all in rapid succession—as I stood gazing, marveling at what I perceived as wings. Though not the wings of any Earth-bound creature.

They were angels. Imperfect angels. Would-be saviors.

"You can't escape us so easily," thundered a voice.

I discerned the words as coming from the reddish one in

the middle. My long-range vision focused on him, his face, as his eyes narrowed.

In the split second before it came, I expected the thin ray of light but had no time to evade its path, couldn't help but scream as my left shoulder and arm seemed to erupt in flames.

Even if I'd had more time to react, evading wouldn't have been on the list—only adjusting my stance. When the second ray came, I did just that, allowing the beam to catch me on just the right spot on my right forearm. The crystals absorbed all the radiation, recycled, and redelivered the ray, redoubling it, tripling it, into a thicker beam, catching the red one in the midsection.

There was no scream, but the beam knocked him back a bit.

I gave half a thought to my next move when, with blazing speed, the dark-green feminine one swooped down in an arc toward me and landed a blow to my midsection that knocked me back, sent me tumbling what had to be several dozen feet.

I was surprised that the wind wasn't knocked out of me but, regaining my footing, soon realized that she'd just been setting me up to rain blows on me: a series of punches, smacks, chops, and kicks coming from every side and so fast that my body was physically unable to fall down or even slump.

Her blasts were plentiful with pain. I felt as if I'd been caught up in a dry whirlpool of swirling lightning bolts and rusty-nail clusters. My ribs should've been cracked, many other bones broken. The crystals kept them strong and helped rapidly heal anything that became too damaged. Still, I could hardly catch my breath, let alone use any to express the torment I felt.

But I'd been through enough in my life. And I'd had therapy. When blows came this fast, this hard, this unrelenting, I'd learned how to regard it as static—a rough, irritating snowstorm background for meditation. Focus.

As she attempted to pulp my body, I focused on what she wasn't doing.

Her wings managed to stay out of her way as she moved. Those glorious wings that were so much more than decoration or equipment enabling flight. She wasn't using them. I would.

As she worked to render my body as anonymous as any unidentifiable corpse, I focused on my body's uniqueness, the crystals, focusing them on drawing light and energy from those flaming wings—the emotional energy of hope and hate and a further variety—recycling them all. Then I let my intuition run its show.

When she went for a blow to my head, I blocked and retaliated with spins, kicks, and windmills—my arms and legs thrusting out blades of glorious fire—burning her, hurting her, forcing her backward, eliciting hollers and screams when that tactic failed. Finally, she leaped back and upward, returning to hover high up in the air.

This place—*my* place, invaded—was, in part, a construct of light. Here, strangeness lived. I'd no doubt these three would have been powerful on the surface of Reality—the familiar realm of space and time—but here, their abilities were stronger, far stronger than they would've been in the original field of awakening or any other part of familiar Earth. And so were mine.

I figured I, too, could take flight, just high enough to hover and mix it up with them at their level.

But as I ran toward them, just before I leaped, the red one gestured toward me with both arms, hurling me into a blizzard of lasers. Solid light pelted me, ripping and gnawing at my body like fire-fueled piranhas, slashing and burning.

Screaming, I collapsed. But I didn't hit the ground. The

light handled me so fiercely, so violently, I was several feet from the ground, tossing and turning and screeching in midair.

My screams increased in volume as my body took control, doing what it could to absorb the swirling lightning strikes, capturing them and recycling them, manipulating them into something harmful, poisonous, deadly to their complacent source.

Before I realized it, I was ascending higher into the air at an angle, toward the red one, carrying the blizzard of light with me. Shock marred his face as he tried to back away, but I was already within range to hurl and surround him in curlicues that struck at him, whipping and thrashing, every lash (I now consciously ensured) feeling to him like the coldest ice or the hottest fire.

I noticed the pale-blue one making a move. I turned in his direction, readying a thick and direct beam toward his head. But he was quicker.

In less than an eye's blink, using the crystals in my skin, the blue one had mapped out constellations on my body and lit them, sending me screeching down toward the ground in excruciating pain as I had flash-fried visions of strange gods and weirder goddesses slaying giant, unnamable beasts.

During my descent, I'd just enough awareness of my surroundings to note the green one tossing a barrage of hateful squiggles at me, a deranged celebrant's confetti—stinging, multihued lights, disorienting me while biting and crushing, cutting and digging. A multitude of fiery ants' mandibles went to work on me before I hit the ground, hard, landing on my back.

I couldn't move. They didn't relent.

Descending upon me, the three attacked at once, submitting my body to a barrage of whips, balls, and spears of light. But these assaults were new, inflicting far less damage externally than internally. With each hit, I experienced a blinking range of emotions, each of them intended—and working—to increase a sense of self-loathing.

Once the three landed, surrounding me, they likely suspected I wouldn't want to move, even if I could. They ceased their assault, relishing their victory. In turn, I weakly observed each of them—them and the creatures crawling about their bodies. Bees, ants, and spiders. All of them busy, scurrying, working on these three beings. Imperfect, yet works in progress.

I saw the three in a new light: three exalted living beings as fertile ground. They weren't finishing me off. They weren't trying to eradicate me. They wanted to subsume what I had in my body.

But I wasn't finished with my body yet. Wasn't finished with my life yet.

Didn't want to be. Couldn't be. This was my space. My realm. My slice of Reality. Something truly, if only temporarily, my own.

I struggled to sit up, only managing to roll to my side.

I heard cackling, chuckling. Derisive laughter coming from the atmosphere itself rather than the three.

Shakily, in searing pain, I managed to push myself to my knees.

Two of them—the blue one and the red one—stood before me in my range of vision. The green one was behind me.

I managed to bring my left knee out from under me, moving it in front of me, planting my foot firmly, ready to push up, fight back.

"... You won't take ... what's mine ..."

"No," said the blue one.

"We're taking back what's ours," said the red one.

"Now"—from behind me, the green one spoke—"let's cover your shame."

I turned at the waist, preparing to thrust myself toward the green one, hoping to grab and embrace her, absorbing all the hate she could give while recycling it, redoubling it, tripling it, giving it back in a manner that would be toxic to her entire existence.

But I was stopped, straightened, levitated beyond my own control. My arms hung at my side, my feet dangled, and my eyes watched as the air became suffused with worms. The same kind I had seen before, only now amassed in one tight area. Thousands of them.

I was pinched, picked at. Gradually, I'd the sensation of multilimbed insects crawling all over my bare body, irritating and agitating various sections. Itching, throbbing . . . Some of those sections attempted to leap up from my body, turn inside out. The edges of such patches oozed mucus—bubbling, acidic . . .

I saw none of it but felt it all intensely. Felt them completing their invasion, their outright takeover of my shelter, of my space. Of me. My will.

All I could see, and quite clearly, was the cloud of worms producing their silk in abundance. The thin strands were doubled, tripled, and thickened further as they drew to my body like a magnet.

I understood. As quickly as it was happening, I comprehended that what I'd seen crawling on the three had moved to my body and gotten to work at lightning speed, weaving a cloak. A robe. An ever-tailored, ever-tightening, rapidly constricting garment that squeezed my midsection, restricting the movements of my arms and legs even as I gave it my all, fighting as hard as I could to use what was still available to me while I still had the chance.

But joints wouldn't bend. Muscles wouldn't flex. Even the crystals were nullified. The flow of blood, stopped—followed soon after by my thoughts.

AFTER AN UNKNOWN PERIOD of absolutely nothing, I was conscious of standing.

My arms at my side. My chin tilted upward. My eyes were open, but a haze clouded my vision.

I was clothed, but my arms were bare. A slight breeze tickled across my forearms and cheeks.

Hesitant to move, I relied on my ears to try to get my bearings. They took in the roar of a distant ocean. Nothing else.

Slowly, the haze wafted away. My vision sharpened. I found myself gazing at the top of the arch—that damned weedy arch from my wedding. The red and white flowers seemed especially vivid against the gray sky above.

I lowered my chin. I was less than a dozen paces away from the arch. Presently, no one was under it. Beyond it, a field of golden grass led to the edge of the cliff. Down below, the sea.

Even though its waves were the only sounds to reach my ears, I knew I wasn't alone.

Bracing myself, I turned around and, lips parted, gazed upon all the men and women seated for the ceremony: two columns of rows, a wide aisle between. All of them wore the faces of the three.

A glance down at my person confirmed what I'd already guessed. I was in the wedding dress. Not the original but the fetishized dress that had so recently been woven for me. A constricting yet sheer white dress adorned with amber-fringed ruffles and lace. The creepy crawlies that had woven it had gone all out.

I wasn't sure what to do. The "guests" all gazed at me. Immobile. Not speaking. Not even blinking. There was nowhere to run. This was another realm just slightly removed from the surface of Reality. In part, a construct of light. But not one that I had constructed. I had even less control here than I'd had in the previous realm.

At once, my attention was pulled to the end of the aisle, directly opposite me, where a patch of air maybe two feet in diameter acquired a purplish hue and shimmered as if harboring a cloud of gnats. Gradually the patch grew, took on dimensions, until it appeared as a rose, half a dozen feet in diameter, a giant violet flower's head, stemless.

I gaped at the spectacle, made no sound or movement as dragonfly-winged scorpions, dozens of them, emerged from deep within the folds. They remained on the petals, scuttling about, going to work with their pincers, cutting away portions, perhaps devouring them, leaving black patches in their wake. Within moments, enough had been shorn away so that the black patches became one large beyond-black hole, out of which stepped a man, naked.

The winged scorpions carried what remained of the giant flower forward, draping the nude figure. The critters then landed and scuttled about, tailoring what remained of the violet rose with amazing speed and skill until the smiling man was clothed in violet and gray vestments. I paid the scorpions little mind as their fluttering wings carried them off and up into the air. My gaze was fixed on the face of the man who no longer had purplish-gray skin but was overly familiar.

I'd no control over this environment. It was all his. But I wagered I had some control over my body—limited, undoubtedly. After all, I was here for a reason. I possessed something that required my assent to give. I still had some measure of free will, free thought and free movement. So I set the crystals to work, drawing in as much light and energy as I could.

"Ah . . ." The man garbed in violet and gray looked me up and down, then grinned as his eyes met mine. "The trappings of the skin . . ."

He walked toward me, his hands behind his back.

"That's what most people see when they see you. When they see a woman. A man. Pretty. Handsome. Dazzling. But how many see the soul? How many can truly glimpse even a portion? No makeup, no clothes, no skin . . . How pretty would a man, how handsome a woman—how dazzling would *you* be to others if you were shorn of your trappings? How tough? How clever or smart beyond the words you've learned, memorized?"

Those seated in the rows on either side of him remained immobile as he passed them. Like mannequins. I moved only a few inches, squaring up with him, my eyes narrowing as he closed the distance between us.

"I'll admit"—he nodded—"you made a very impressive attempt at an escape. Put up a much better fight than expected. But now you've realized it's futile."

Just a few more steps.

"Having control over a piece of your soul, the witch possesses and affords you certain advantages. But you now realize ours are greater. Your brain? That lump of grayish brown between your ears? It is just an overripe piece of fruit. *Mushy.* And me, I am the worm in that rotting apple. Wherever you think to go from now on, no matter where in Reality, I will know, and we will follow. On and on. Until you give me what I have so gentlemanly *asked* you to give—you *tart.*"

From my eyes, I released two twisting beams, on and on, a double helix of light that fired directly into his eyes—until he shut them, lunged forward, and backhanded my face. A fierce blow. But I neither fell nor stumbled as his other hand was quick to thrust forward, clasp around my throat, and squeeze.

"*Trash*. There's nothing you can do to hurt me. But as you can feel, that doesn't work in reverse."

He released his grip, letting my body fall to the golden ground.

"Now, if you're done, let us get on with the ceremony. And let's do our best to make it work this time."

He moved past me toward the arch. I lay on my side, gasping and coughing, attempting to regain my breath before I got to my feet.

The light from my eyes hadn't been to hurt him. Yes, I knew that would have been futile, so it hadn't been my intention. Instead, the light had been to read him, his thoughts, whatever I could get.

It wasn't a lot, but I managed to capture just enough. Enough to know how to wake the girl without the doctor's assistance. Enough to know why I kept coming back to wedding ceremonies. Enough to have a good idea of how to free myself—from his grasp and from the witch-girl's.

I pushed up to a knee then heaved myself to a standing position. He glared at me, but I kept my eyes soft as I took my position.

The ceremony on his mind was a perversion of a wedding, but no less of a ritual. A magickal one. Rather than the groom standing before him, waiting for the bride to appear and make her way down the aisle, he, as the officiant, would perform a ceremony with a stand-in for a bride—*me*—and if all was successful, a groom would appear, bearing no rings or vows but ready and willing to divulge explicit details on where in Reality the doctor was hiding and how to get to him.

I had no intention of letting that happen.

As I once suspected and now knew, *Love* was the answer.

The answer and the key to me being free, to me being whole. And when seemingly cut off from it, I could cultivate it.

The officiant began the ceremony, speaking to me about me, then to the others seated, and then seemingly to the atmosphere itself, weaving increasingly esoteric words through and around us all, any who could hear, anything that could receive sound, acknowledge, and perhaps respond.

Beyond his voice, the air hummed. The ground beneath us vibrated. The officiant, I, and those seated trembled slightly.

I closed my eyes. Sight was of no use to me at the moment. It was actually a hindrance.

I let a somewhat familiar urge build, careful to take my time yet not to take too long to feel the rhythm of my surroundings, to fall in sync, and then to break away.

I opened my eyes as I backpedaled away from the arch, away from the officiant. I whirled into the wide aisle, and I danced.

And *danced*—allowing the flowing movements to stir memories of when I last did so freely, happily, cultivating love within, a love of my truest self, while also getting in greater touch with this slice of Reality around me, one primarily of light.

I ignored the scenery, focusing on vibrations. Felt them. Made them my own as, within, I tapped into a deep understanding of my needs. I embraced desire and destiny. Being true to oneself—appreciating one's own true worth—was essential to being able to love and be loved by others.

As I danced, my dress stained and unraveled, spinning off golden silk strands that slid in and out of invisibility depending on how the light hit them.

And, as anticipated, the guests got antsy at my act of self-loving defiance. Disapproving, they moved to engage me, to stop me, perhaps to force me back to my position.

But, as intuited, my body had a few surprises, some stored scenarios, a selection of vivid images fueled by memories of recent events. My memories—those powerful lights within me—were the key. The key to unlocking pure, unbridled joy.

Dancing to my own beat, falling deep into my own rhythm, I emitted dazzling colors, bright and dull, an entire range, which rapidly coalesced, became holograms, taking the shape of men and women—not generics, but the kinky figures from where I'd so recently spent an evening and night. Some were those I'd seen. Others whom I didn't recognize must have seen me while I was awake, while I was conscious, or maybe even afterward.

Whatever, whichever, that didn't matter now. They were here now, images vivid enough and real enough to physically engage with the masses of guests who attempted to converge on me but wound up indulging in the most deranged fantasies. Sexual adventures and tortures of every imagining.

Ears, lips, eyelids, nostrils, nipples, genitalia, parcels of skin—all of them and more portals to the senses, all of them and more belonging to the wedding guests were dressed and decorated—pierced, pinched, clamped, tickled, or otherwise affected. The would-be mob of my attackers, the mass of imperfect versions, their sensory experiences went to and flew beyond those of the average human being.

Superior experiences? Maybe.

All I experienced, felt, understood was they were being converted. The construct of light around me was falling under my control.

And I danced. Denuding myself further, I danced on.

The violet-and-gray-clad officiant frantically tried to find his way through the frenzied mass of writhing, twisting bodies: a free and clear way to me, to grab me, snatch me up and carry me back to my place to submit to my duty, to play my role. But he got too close to the merrymakers, close enough to be snatched up and quickly violated in horrific ways.

As the gang of violent deviants subsumed him, I—mostly naked—stopped dancing and took off running. Toward the cliff. Beyond it, the ocean down below came into greater view. A horizon-spanning mass of turbulent, midnight-blue waters. But I didn't slow. I transferred the passion I had for dancing to running, increasing my speed until, so very near the edge, I leaped, thrusting myself forward, inevitably arcing downward.

Ignoring the near-total darkness into which I was leaping, I closed my eyes, gave myself over to the total darkness within, letting the crystals work.

After uncounted seconds, pinpricks of twinkling white appeared. Two, a few, then many more until I saw an entire field of white specks floating against a black background.

Among the hundreds, one speck flared in bright pink, assuming the shape of a keyhole. Reflexively, my attention was pulled toward it, focused on it until I saw an image of another time and place. The image tugged at me, gently, at something deep inside my being—maybe the core of my soul. But I stayed put as the keyhole swiftly shrunk back to a white pinprick.

The process repeated multiple times, rapidly, until just the right image pulled me forward and *through*.

I CAME to in what I assumed was a sitting position, planted atop a table or platform that I assumed was circular. I'd no choice but to make assumptions. I couldn't move. Couldn't feel my body at all.

Whatever I was on was rotating, slowly, giving me a gradual view of my immediate, nearly eye-level surroundings: lanterns and ropy branches of white flowers and greenery trailing downward, no farther than an arm's length from me, all of them suspended from something above me at which I could only guess.

Beyond all the drapery, on one side of me were a modest-size two-level house and other structures one might find on a family farm. On all the other sides of me were rolling hills, and rows upon rows of trellises abundant with vines. Grapevines.

I was in a vineyard. It was a sunny day. And, once again, I was in a unique prison cell of someone's diabolical design.

A variety of flowers' fragrances perfumed the air. Yet competing—and winning—was something sweeter, heavier. Sugary. A scent pleasant and vaguely familiar but nothing I could connect with what I was seeing around me.

I saw no one. Heard nothing but birdsong coming from the distant trees at the periphery of the vineyard and, closer to me, those large plants adjacent to the buildings.

Alone in nature—until, after about three and a half rotations, I heard the sound of a door closing behind me. In half a rotation, I saw figures approaching from the direction of the house. Carmilla and eight of her acolytes.

The eight young men and women were garbed in suits and dresses. Attire suitable for a ceremony. A ceremony that Carmilla made plain by her priestess garb.

All nine were grinning and carrying large knives or similar long and sharp tools, sunlight glinting off the polished silver.

As they neared, I tried to speak—to ask questions, to protest whatever the ravenous looks in their eyes were hinting they were about to do—but I had nothing to speak with. Nothing that I could access anyway.

But I was seeing. I was smelling. I was hearing. I was doing it all somehow.

The nine surrounded my platform, still grinning. Carmilla

hummed a chuckle, then said, "Ah, pretty Jenny . . . Are you ready for your big day?"

I tried but could say nothing.

"Ready or not, the party is ready for you. But first, I'd like to thank you for giving us the solutions we desire. Thanks to you, we no longer need the doctor. Thanks to you, we will have the formula."

I didn't know what she was going on about and certainly didn't want to. As I rotated, I got a good view of all their faces, all their expressions. Even as I listened to the witch, I could read the words on her acolytes' closed lips. I would have shuddered if I could.

"And thanks to me working with you, the Trinfecta played right into my hands. Though I must say, they gave their all.

"They sweetened and softened you up, got you to a better position than I could have on my own—though it's not humble-bragging to say I did my part as well . . .

"I knew they wouldn't have you. You wouldn't let them any more than you'd let me. But you've been put in a condition and position where you are now *mine*."

All I had left were my thoughts. And I wondered now, more seriously—more seriously than I'd ever considered anything—whether I could exist in two different states at two different times and yet somehow remain fully connected. But I altered it, colored the conditioning, wondering if I could truly exercise my divinity by flowing to a different state, at a different time, connecting the present self to another and leaving this one behind.

"Ah . . ." Carmilla drew out the sound, at once purring and chiding. "You seemed worried about the future." She was half-right. Some witch. "You should know better than that. All the therapies you've had, all the therapists that have guided you . . .

You should well know: your true future cannot be embraced in fear."

It made no sense. But nothing the witch said to me now would make any sense. I was working, on my way . . .

"By the way, I've returned the portion of your soul I've been keeping safe from you. I no longer need it. And neither do you. Your body is now in a completely different phase of matter than what you're accustomed to. And you have absolutely no more control. I, and my most faithful acolytes, will handle matters from here."

In unison, they raised their instruments and dug in, stabbing, cutting, carving, inflicting the deepest wounds.

They would have their ceremonial dessert, consuming what was left of my physical self, satiating themselves on my transformed vessel and celebrating as they moved onward with some magickal scheme. But to me, it was no matter.

I now knew myself. Completely. And I was halfway to my final home.

I MATERIALIZED IN A DAMP, dark parking lot, recognizing it immediately, even before laying sight on the bar's name glowing in neon above the entrance.

I moved. I couldn't exactly call it running, though. More like swiftly gliding through the air with my feet only briefly, lightly touching the wet asphalt.

"Feet" may not have been accurate either. My body was different from what I'd so lately grown accustomed to. I'd discarded the shell, left it to be consumed by the witch-girl and her goons. Now I felt like the inchoate substance of passion enveloped in an otherworldly silk, layered and molded in a vague shape tending toward a genderless human adult.

I felt not even a hint of pain as I shoved myself through the bar's doors. Though I entered with force and verve, it may as well have been a clandestine entry. No one noticed.

Everyone was levitating. Twenty-three were naked. Only the devil wore clothes. Only he was conscious. *Doctor Linkins.* I saw his face clearly now. And I clearly saw what he was doing.

He levitated several feet above the floor, his legs pressed together, his toes pointed downward like water diviners, his back slightly arched, and his arms moving as if he were conducting a symphony.

In fact, he was.

Streamers of light flew from his body to his victims. Pieces of skin were peeled off like the thinnest of tissue paper, seemingly discarded, fluttering about like blown autumn leaves, only to be reattached while other skin swatches began the same cycle. Bodies went translucent. Their insides, a patchwork of hues, flashing and dulling and defying any place on the primary color spectrum. Organs were rearranged, removed, then replaced.

The doctor was dissecting people in midair, searching for and attempting to collect his precious red ice. All the while, the bodies emitted lines of sung words—fragments of songs and poems—like air escaping from pierced, deflating balloons.

And I (me then) was in closest proximity to him.

I had once sought to be placed in a scenario where I could exact revenge. Now here (and there) I was, ready to take it even further.

The silken sheath of my vessel unraveled and ignited as I rushed toward the doctor. His head snapped in my direction, but he'd no time, no space to evade. Burning with dark desire, I engulfed him. He fought—struggled and cursed—but he couldn't shake me.

He danced. I made him dance, bedeviling him like an aerosol of toxic mist glistening and fastening to his body, sinking into his skin, evoking an agonized scream from him that rose and fell, halted and began again, never ceasing completely.

His skin turned inside out as he evoked his own inner power and abilities to fight back, to blank me out. But I would not be extinguished, not until I redeemed the others. The bartender was beyond gone, but twenty-three would be saved.

My passionate self further darkened as I used the bad doctor's powers against him. Our inferno of inholy fire spread as different rays of light emanated from us, connected to all the others—consuming them, breaking them down to their essentials while slowly teleporting their remade vessels forward in time—establishing a web of light with the doctor and me at the center.

This devil . . . He'd deemed himself the lord of the flying, buzzing memories of those he'd assaulted, dissected, and sought to manipulate. Retribution was in the offing. His victims' memories traveled along the web of light like flies not hindered but aided by the construct of electromagnetic radiation, not bothered but hungrily drawn to the spidery dancing doctor, legs and arms stretched out, bending and waving every which way.

Those fragments of songs and poems the victims had emitted began again and rapidly lengthened into verses, verses that strengthened as I drew the victims' memories, pieces of their clustered souls, and hardened them. Crystallized them. I then further refined, created gemstones, sparkling.

The detritus—flashes of lives never to be fully lived—were flung outward in space, forward in time, destined to strike the surface of Reality like lightning and inhabit the recreated bodies of our selves, doomed simulacrums. Our truest selves would reside elsewhere.

All of us—the refined essence of our unique beings—were erased from the surface of Reality and placed elsewhere by my will.

I could not destroy the doctor. But I—we—could keep him, neutralize him, hide him on another level of Reality removed from the common concept of time, a bleached nether region where no one could ever discover him. We would see that he forever remained imprisoned, an impossible puzzle in white space, the focus of a configuration of sparkling black diamonds —the twenty-three of us, his one-time victims—shining in a complicated sequence that only we understood and that he'd never decode.

Our twinkling regimen would forever blind him, bind him, remind him of his never-to-be-fulfilled promise. His deserved punishment.

Conscientious obsolescence . . . Marriage. A respectable life. The rat race of finding one's place and earning just enough money to sustain and subsist. That had once been the fire deep within me. I may be a monster for assuming the others' inner fire—trapping it, manipulating it, repurposing it—assuming I knew it well enough and assuming it for my own (*our best*) purposes. But this is what it would take to prevent a greater evil from having free reign on Reality's surface.

I sacrificed myself, and I enlisted the sacrifice of others (may they forgive) to fulfill my divine mission, to prevent the doctor from further experiments, from further engaging in his atrocious plans for humanity.

All twenty-three of us who died in the bar that night found ourselves in a communal art, trapping a devil in a design his sober self was far too clever to ever devise.

This, I loved.

ABOUT THE SERIES

When their bodies are overwhelmed by an onslaught of parasites that feed on blood and light, most victims of the White Fire Virus die quickly but in excruciating pain. They could be considered the lucky ones. Those who survive continue to live on in physical and psychological torment; they also find themselves endowed with a range of supernatural abilities. Many of these survivors consider themselves angels, potential saviors of humanity. Others want nothing less than the death of God. And there are a few who are even more ambitious.

With stories set in a world where humankind's twisted fantasies and most disturbing nightmares have manifested as pulsing, hard-edged realities, *Eve of Light* is a dark fantasy horror series unlike any other. Mind-bending and provocative. Dark fiction at its weirdest.

The Core Novels

BloodLight: The Apocalypse of Robert Goldner
Lilith's Arithmetic: The Revelations of Artemisia Wright
Broken Angels (Eve of Light, Book I)
Divinities, Entangled (Eve of Light, Book II)

The Deviant-Hunter Stories

Deviant-Hunter: Blood Oath

Deviant-Hunter, Killer of Saints
Deviant-Hunter's Sabbath

<u>Other Stories on the Fringe</u>
The Lark
Heaven's Gun
White Fire
Rogue Beauty
FoolKillers
Knotty & Ice
Influx

EVE OF LIGHT STORY ORDER

Although it is recommended that readers begin the series with either a standalone story or *Broken Angels*, there is no suggested reading order. What follows, however, is a list of where the current stories generally fall within the timeline of events.

The Lark
Lilith's Arithmetic: The Revelations of Artemisia Wright
BloodLight: The Apocalypse of Robert Goldner
Heaven's Gun
White Fire
Rogue Beauty
Deviant-Hunter: Blood Oath
Deviant-Hunter, Killer of Saints
Deviant-Hunter's Sabbath
Broken Angels (Eve of Light, Book I)
FoolKillers
Knotty & Ice
Divinities, Entangled (Eve of Light, Book II)
Influx

ABOUT THE AUTHOR

Harambee K. Grey-Sun is the author of several novels, novellas, and short stories, including *Hero Zero, Colder Than Ice,* and the story collection *Blind Dates.* For more information about his books and ongoing projects, please visit www.harambeegrey-sun.com.

ALSO BY HARAMBEE K. GREY-SUN

<u>Standalone Stories</u>

Colder Than Ice

<u>The *GRACE OTHERWISE* Series</u>

Blind Dates

<u>The *HERO ZERO* Series</u>

Hero Zero

BY HARAMBEE GREY-SUN

<u>Poetry</u>

Spring's Fall (Autumn Numbers * Book I)

Wine Songs, Vinegar Verses

Trinity & Its Twin